Four Seasons of Love

Four Seasons of Love

A Romance Anthology

Divine Garden Press

Published by Divine Garden Press
PO Box 371
Soperton, GA 30457
www.divinegardenpress.com
ISBN-13: 978-0615795683
ISBN-10: 0615795684
Cover Design: A'ndrea J. Wilson
Cover Photo: ©Katrina Brown | 123rf.com

Contents

Autumn

AUTUMN ACADEMICS AND AFFAIRS

The Hope & Bliss Story: Part 1

By A'ndrea J. Wilson

Victoria secretly hated her job. She used to love it, but every semester that passed brought more demanding students and an even more demanding administration. Each time she got an email or letter from the Department of Academic Affairs, she cringed wondering what systematic change would make her have to work twice as hard for the same paycheck. The only reasons she stayed was because she had grown accustomed to her three-bedroom townhouse and her luxurious, late model Chrysler 300; she couldn't afford either without being on payroll at Rochester State University. Not only that, but she loved the looks on people's faces when she told them that she was a college professor.

"Oh! You look so young!" they said in shock, as they reclassified her in their minds. She would watch their eyes; she could see her name being moved up from NOBODY to PEOPLE WE RESPECT.

"I am," she'd respond with a polite smile. In her mind, she always questioned why people assumed a college professor had to be an ancient looking man, dressed in a tweed suit with a salt and pepper beard, who rambled about theory all day. Why couldn't society redefine a higher education instructor to be a curvy woman with short, curly, auburn hair, who typically wore cotton t-shirts and blue denim jeans?

She might not have looked the part, but she definitely played it. Just as summer vacation was getting good, and the stress from spring semester was rolling off of her shoulders, the fall semester returned, and so did her four sections of undergraduate Human Sexuality and her Monday night graduate-level, Treatment Planning course. Yes, she taught Human Sexuality, but the course was nothing like it sounded. She was an Assistant Professor of Psychology, and her Human Sexuality course was textbook only. The last thing she wanted were students complaining to the dean that some video or discussion in the class made them feel uncomfortable. Therefore, she kept her lectures strictly scientific: the human body, reproduction, development, illness. That was it. Of course, every term, a few perverted students attempted to make sly comments to jazz up the material, but she quickly shut them down and continued on with her academic lessons.

It was her first day back, and she hadn't yet settled into her office when the semester's first dilemma arose. As she dropped her purse onto the desk and sank down into her leather chair, her office door flew open, and an unknown man, carrying a big cardboard box, barged in.

"Excuse me! Don't you know how to knock?" she exclaimed, completely annoyed by his intrusion.

He placed the heavy looking box down on the empty desk on the other side of the office. "Sorry. You must be Dr. Victoria Hope. I've heard wonderful things about you. I'm Byron Bliss. Dr. Byron Bliss."

He extended his hand to Victoria, and she shook it halfheartedly. "Nice to meet you, Byron. I'm sure you're a nice person and a colleague I should probably know, but I don't understand why you are in my office."

He grinned, revealing the most alluring dimple in his right cheek. "Oh. Academic Affairs must not have had the chance to tell you yet. I'll be sharing this office with you. They're doing renovation work to Baxter Hall, so they had to move me. I guess your office is actually a double, so they put me in here. Sorry if my being here will inconvenience you in any way."

Victoria took a moment to size him up. She had to admit to herself that he was attractive. Smooth, taffy-colored skin, chestnut eyes, tall, a solid build as if he used to play football back in college, and that hard to resist dimple. Yeah, he was what she and her friends called *scrumptious*, the kind of guy that you could easily overindulge in, sort of like eating chocolate cake.

Although he was a handsome specimen, Victoria (or Vicki like her family and friends called her) wasn't interested. Life was overwhelming enough; she didn't want or need any additional extracurricular activities. As it was, her job was barely tolerable, she had just dismissed her last flunky boyfriend, Scott, for being unfaithful, and her family had decided to host Thanksgiving dinner at her house without her consent, regardless of the fact that she couldn't cook! She desperately needed to make it through the semester with as less drama as possible. No, there would not, could not, be any taste-testing of Dr. Bliss.

Instead of returning his smile, she rolled her eyes. "No, they did not tell me. Academic Affairs never tells me or even asks me anything. I guess I don't have a choice in the matter, so make yourself comfortable."

He nodded and began to remove his laptop and other items from the cardboard box. "You know, maybe our schedules are opposing and we won't need to use the office at the same time. I am sure we can work something out. What do you teach?"

"Human Sexuality and Treatment Planning. Mondays, Wednesdays, and Fridays with office hours between classes. You?"

"Business Sustainability and Operations Management. Same days."

"Fantastic," she said sarcastically. "Any other good news you have for me?"

"Uh, I just saved a lot of money on my car insurance using Geico." He smiled.

"Oh, a funny guy, huh?"

"It works with the students."

"I bet." She swirled around to face her desk, nonverbally letting him know that their conversation was over. She hated to come off as icy, yet she wasn't in the mood for small talk. Plus, the less she knew about Dr. Bliss, the less likely she would end up violating her own rule against fraternizing with male colleagues. *Pretend he's not here*, she thought to herself as she tried with all of her might to ignore the cutest man on campus who happened to be sitting directly behind her.

At Rochester State University, professors were required to return to work a week and a half before students started classes. The week was full of pointless meetings and faculty development seminars aimed at getting everyone on one accord for the school year. Vicki dreaded these activities, hating that the school's administration continued to give the same information out over and over again. She'd rather be at home, curled up with a good book or shoe shopping with her identical twin sister Vivian. Instead, on the third day back to work, at 12:30 PM, she found herself in a faculty luncheon that focused on student safety.

The chicken was dry, the salad dressing was sparse, and the only good thing about the luncheon was that she got to sit next to her good friend and colleague, Nancy Watkins.

"Who is that?" Nancy said as she leaned closer to Vicki, but kept her eyes firmly on the man who had caught her attention.

"Who?" Vicki said before following Nancy's stare. "Oh, that's Dr. Bliss. The guy I was telling you about. The one that infiltrated my office."

"That's Dr. Bliss? Oh my! Well, if you don't want to shack up with him, I will."

"Hush."

"Do I detect a hint of jealousy?" Nancy teased.

"No, you don't. You can have him. I am so not interested."

"Come on now. You mean to tell me that you don't find him the least bit attractive? The man is practically model material. I would love to hang a poster of him on my bedroom wall."

Vicki gasped. "Would you stop mentally fornicating with him? I didn't say that he wasn't attractive. He's very good looking, but that's not the point."

"Then what's the point?"

Lost for words, Vicki hesitated while watching Byron Bliss take his seat just as the university's president approached the podium. "The point is . . . President Brown is getting ready to speak. Stop being rude and be quiet."

Nancy giggled. "Mm hmm. That's what I thought."

Despite Nancy's insinuations, Vicki was not interested in Dr. Bliss, or so she told herself. She managed to get through the rest of the pre-semester period and into the first two weeks of classes without having to spend too much time cramped in her office with her new officemate. She did so by making every excuse to leave when he came in and return after he'd left back out. She had no clue why she felt the need to run from him, but something within her told her that it was best that she maintained her distance. He reminded her of several of the men whom she had dated who were too sexy for their own good. Most of the time, they knew they were handsome and played it to their advantage, breaking hearts along the way. When she was in her twenties, it was cool to get swept away by some hunk, but she was in her thirties now, which meant she was way too old to be falling for the same tricks.

"Don't forget that your papers on attraction are due next class and make sure they are formatted in APA. If you don't know APA, you better figure it out before you turn in those papers because I am deducting ten percent for anything formatted incorrectly," she said firmly to the students in one of her Human Sexuality courses before dismissing them.

The students groaned in complaint, but she shrugged at them to demonstrate her lack of sympathy. She had become exhausted by their laziness and unwillingness to work hard for their education. It appeared that the only method that worked in getting them to follow instructions was threatening their grades, so she used the approach guiltlessly.

Vicki collected her binders and headed to her office to get some grading done before her final class of the day. She prayed that Byron wouldn't be there, but her prayer went unanswered. She walked into the office and found him sitting at his desk, conversing with a female student.

"Hello, Dr. Bliss," she said evenly, trying to keep the resentment out of her voice.

"Hi, Dr. Hope," he responded cheerfully before turning his attention back to the young woman.

Vicki quickly assessed the woman and cut her eyes at her. She couldn't have been a day older than twenty-one, yet was wearing a skirt that barely covered her unmentionables. Vicki never understood why women disrespected themselves by acting promiscuous and thinking it would get them the men they desired. No matter the man, they were all the same. Once a man got what he wanted from a woman, he was on his way to the next conquest. None of them were different, including Dr. Bliss; she was sure of it.

"From now on, slow down when you're reading the material and taking the quizzes. You'll do fine. It's not as hard as it looks, Trish," Byron said to the girl as he stood up, indicating to her that their meeting was over.

"Okay. Thanks so much, Dr. Bliss. I just don't want to fail this class. This is my senior year, and I have to graduate on time," the young woman replied.

It took everything within Vicki not to laugh out loud. The girl was obviously playing him. What student cared so much about her grades this early in the semester? No, that's not how it worked. Students were notorious for playing around over half of the semester and then waiting until a few weeks before finals to come crying about their grades. This young woman was pulling the old damsel in distress card on Byron, and he was too full of himself to know the difference.

As soon as the student left the office, Vicki spun around in her chair and gave Byron an annoyed glare. "Seriously? Tell me you really didn't fall for that," she mocked him.

Dr. Bliss looked over at her and laughed. "Fall for what?"

"That whole I'm-so-concerned-about-my-grades performance. You and I both know that students could care less at this point. Most of them believe they have plenty of time to fix whatever mistakes they make early in the semester. The only ones who really care are the overachievers who have to make an A on everything or their world comes crashing down. And trust me, that little girl who just left here is definitely not an overachiever."

"Wow, you've got it all figured out, huh?"

"It doesn't take long to know the routine."

"What happened to you?"

"What do you mean?"

"Why are you so cynical?"

"Excuse me?"

"You heard me. What did the school or some student do to you to make you so negative? Yeah, that student probably has a crush on me and was just using her failed quiz as an excuse to get close to me, but if I can use the opportunity to help her improve academically, so be it. That's our job, to motivate and develop these students by any means necessary."

Vicki shook her head in disapproval. "OK, Malcolm X. If you're done with your civil rights slash enthusiastic educator speech, I'll get back to loathing my job and counting down the days until Thanksgiving break like most overworked and underpaid educators."

Byron let out an unexpected laugh, causing Vicki to frown at him in disdain.

"What's so funny?"

"You are. As much as your misery is somewhat comical, it's also very cute."

Vicki held her breath at the recognition of his flirtation. *Did he really just call me cute?* She refused to linger on the thought or even consider that Byron could be attracted to her. Pushing the silly idea aside, she exhaled and turned her back to him.

"So, what excitement is awaiting you during Thanksgiving break?" he continued as if she were still facing him.

She huffed, irritated that he couldn't take her hint. As she flipped through her grade book she replied, "Only the seasonal joys of hosting Thanksgiving dinner with a bunch of nosey relatives who expect me to cook foods that I don't have the slightest idea of how to make."

"You have such a way with sarcasm, but if you need help with cooking, I used to work as a chef. I can teach you a few holiday recipes."

"Thanks, but no thanks.

"You sure?"

"Yep. Positive."

"All right, I tried. Anyway, I have a meeting so I'm heading out," Byron said as he shoved a few papers into his leather bag and slid it onto his shoulder. "Vicki, try to ease up a bit on the students. They're here because they need us."

Vicki ignored his comment and waved him away. "Goodbye, Byron."

A week and a half later, Vicki entered her office and was surprised to find her nostrils bombarded by the alluring aroma of potato salad, greens, fried chicken, and macaroni and cheese. She was more than surprised to find a Styrofoam container filled with foods she typically only ate on holidays placed strategically on her desk. She figured that the plate was the workings of Dr. Bliss, and she was tempted to return it to his desk, but her stomach grumbled in dispute of the rebellious thought. Hungry and curious, she forked a few of the leafy, seasoned greens into her mouth and moaned in delight. She continued on to sample each of the items in the container, her taste buds in agreement that the food was to die for. She closed her eyes for a second to savor the richness of the food, opening them to find Byron standing across from her wearing a smug grin.

"Good, huh?" he asked, although he could probably tell from her guilty expression that she was in heaven.

Vicki resisted the urge to lick the plastic fork and instead placed it inside the container and closed the box. She wanted to eat the rest, but would have to save it for later. "Ye-yeah. It's quite tasty," she replied, feeling uncomfortable with complimenting him.

"I made it last night for dinner and thought about you, so I brought you some. I figured you should try out my food for yourself before you turn down my offer to help you cook for Thanksgiving, again."

"That's very thoughtful of you, but I don't know if–"

"Listen, I'm sure you're probably used to doing things on your own, but it's OK to get a little help from time to time. Look at it as payment for having to share your office with me."

She had to admit to herself that his food was wonderful and that she needed culinary help badly. As much as she wanted to reject any notion of using his services, the holiday was rapidly approaching, and she still had no game plan on how to resolve her cooking deficiency. She had considered purchasing pre-made food, but her family was old school and would quickly sniff out store-bought food. Her only two options were trying to cook herself which was likely to result in dry turkey and tasteless black-eyed peas or to enlist the help of someone who knew what they were doing . . . someone like Byron.

Cursing herself and the situation under her breath, she gave in, hating the fact that she needed him. "OK, Bryon. You can help me with Thanksgiving dinner," she responding, making it sound as if she was the one doing the favor.

He laughed, most likely at her stubbornness. "Now, that wasn't so hard, was it?"

She gave him a malicious glare, already regretting her decision.

"So we can do this one of two ways. I can either come to your place the morning of Thanksgiving and cook the food for you, or I can start teaching you how to cook now so that you can make everything yourself on Thanksgiving. I have a huge kitchen so it would probably be best for me to teach you at my place."

She let his words replay in her mind. If he came to her house on Thanksgiving, there was a chance that he would run into her family, and she would never hear the end of it. They would want to know who he was and why she wasn't dating him. From that moment on, at every family gathering, they would question her about the good looking professor she let get away. Plus, she never allowed men she knew to meet her family because she feared letting men get too close to her heart. No, coming to her house on Thanksgiving wouldn't work. Vicki dreaded the idea of having to meet with him at his house for cooking lessons, but it was a better choice than bringing him home for the holiday.

"Let's just have you teach me in advance."

"Okay, great. Well, Thanksgiving is a little over a month away, so why don't we get started soon so that you'll have enough time to cook each dish more than once before Turkey Day. If you're free next weekend, you can come by and we'll make . . . maybe we can do a hen, cornbread dressing, and greens."

His plan sounded overwhelming. She couldn't imagine herself cooking any of those items, but for the sake of not looking weak, she said, "Fine."

On Saturday, Vicki wished she would have answered "no" instead. She stood in front of the door to his downtown, loft apartment, debating whether she should ring the bell or run. She wasn't sure what it was about Byron that made her feel so uneasy. He had been nothing but polite and kind to her, yet her defenses went up every time he was around. She wanted to chalk up her hesitancy to still being upset over having to share her office with him, but they were halfway through the semester, and she had already accepted her officemate's presence.

The thought entered her mind that maybe she liked him, but she quickly dismissed it. There was no way that she was interested in Dr. Bliss. Yes, he was charismatic and attractive and intelligent, but he still wasn't her type. But what exactly was her type? She questioned herself about her preferences in men as she stood in front of his door with her hand raised in the air as if she intended to knock, but couldn't find the courage. Before she could make up her mind, the door swung open and a casually dressed Byron Bliss greeted her, looking yummy as usual.

"You made it," he said, as he backed away from the entrance to let her in. "I was going to call to see if you got lost."

She permitted her eyes to scan him critically. He seemed relaxed, too relaxed, wearing a black, fleece, Adidas sweat suit and a pair of flannel slippers. The jacket to the sweat suit was unzipped, exposing a white, cotton t-shirt and smooth brown skin. A wayward thought about him taking off his jacket and revealing his muscular arms crossed her mind. She mentally scolded herself for being a sucker for a good looking man and vowed to control her fantasies, especially those including Byron.

Offering a chilly smile, she entered his loft and allowed him to lead her to the kitchen. Byron had prepped for her visit; the countertop was filled with groceries, seasonings, and cookware for their lesson. Vicki pulled off her jacket, hanging it on the back of a chair nearby.

"OK, we need to get the greens and the hen started because they will take the longest to cook," he said while he began to season the hen. Once the hen was in the oven, he showed her how to cut and clean collard greens. Putting them in a big pot on the stove to cook, he then began to demonstrate making cornbread for the dressing. While they prepared the food, he inserted a Kenny G CD into the player and let the jazzy rhythm become the soundtrack for their cooking lesson.

Vicki was impressed as she watched Byron command control over the kitchen. She never thought domestic work was a turn-on until Byron let her spend several hours in the kitchen with him. Now she finally understood why so many women believed in cooking for their men. Seeing someone create the most enticing smells and delectable entrees could easily serve as a romance enticer. She decided then that she would commit to learning how to cook. Whoever her next beau, he would benefit from her new appreciation of preparing hot meals.

Hours after her arrival at his home, they sat down to enjoy the food for which they had been slaving over half of the day to make. Byron set the table and took the liberty of adding yams and split pea soup to the menu, both which he had cooked the night prior. They ate in silence until Byron finally asked, "So, what do you think?"

"Everything is delicious," she answered after wiping her mouth with a napkin.

"I agree. Was cooking with me as painful as you imagined?"

Vicki laughed. "No, not at all. I hate to admit it, but it was actually nice. Cooking is a lot of work and takes quite a bit of time, but eating food like this is definitely worth it."

"Once again, I agree. So now you know how to make hen, greens, cornbread, and dressing. Next time I will teach you how to fry chicken, bake macaroni and cheese, cook cabbage, and maybe whip up some potato salad. How does that sound?"

"It sounds great, but I am so full right now that I don't want to hear anything about any more food."

Byron chuckled and nodded. "Understood."

Two weeks flew by, and before Vicki knew it, she was back at Byron's loft, learning how to make the soul food she loved most. Their relationship had taken a drastic turn from cordial and polite to authentic and friendly. She was starting to look forward to running into him at the office, and by the second week, they had even grabbed lunch together on three occasions.

As they cooked, Vicki felt comfortable enough with him to tell him about the various family members who would be in attendance at her Thanksgiving dinner. She was expecting approximately thirty relatives to take over her space for the day, leaving behind dirty dishes, mounds of trash, and remnants of the meal that was served. To help ease her clean up concerns, Byron coached her on how to use paper plates, plastic utensils, and foil baking pans to cut down on the dishes to be washed. He also agreed to come to her house the day after Thanksgiving to help straighten her home back up.

Vicki looked at him and sighed. She enjoyed spending time with Byron and appreciated his assistance, but she couldn't seem to wrap her mind around his generosity. "Why are you doing all of this? Don't you have your own Thanksgiving plans? I'm sure you have family or a girlfriend you want to be with on the holiday instead of hanging around and helping me."

Byron slid a pan of macaroni and cheese into the oven and closed the oven's door. Turning around, he leaned against the counter and said, "I'm doing this because you need me. Yes, I have my own Thanksgiving plans. I'll be spending the day with my parents and siblings. And no, I don't have a girlfriend. Any more questions?"

She smirked. "So that's what this is about? You like the idea of me needing you?"

"No, that is not what this is about. This is about helping others. We are supposed to help those in need, and you are in need." Byron chucked and then continued. "However, in all honesty, I do get a small fraction of pleasure out of you needing me."

"Why?"

"Because women like you never want to admit when you need someone, especially a man. It's OK to have needs; it's OK to ask for help. That is how God created us, to lean on each other." Byron walked across the kitchen over to Vicki, stopping so close to her that she unconsciously stepped backwards to give herself more room. He moved even closer, filling the few inches that separated them. "Why won't you admit that you need me?"

She opened her mouth, but no words came out. She wanted to scream at him, push him away, and walk out of the door, but her body wouldn't cooperate. She could smell a hint of his aftershave, hear him breathing in and out, and feel the warmth from his skin as he reached out, tilted her chin upward, and planted a soft kiss on her lips. "Vicki, admit that you need me," he repeated once his lips parted from hers.

Vicki felt weak. Her lips still tingled from the kiss. Butterflies spread throughout her stomach and chest. "I . . ." was all she managed to mumble before he lowered his face to hers and kissed her again.

"Tell me that you need me," he requisitioned once more.

She had to get away from him. He wanted too much too soon. She looked down at her trembling hands. He had an effect on her that no man could ever claim. She felt emotions that she didn't want to feel for him or anyone else. As much as she wanted to give into the passion that was surging up within her, she couldn't trust him or what she was feeling.

"No," she said, finding her voice and words again. "I have to go." Vicki backed away from him, grabbed her coat and hat, and headed out the door, leaving Byron alone with a kitchen full of food.

Vicki sat in her car, trembling over her close encounter with Byron. He was right; she needed him, but that didn't mean she would make herself vulnerable to him. She learned the hard way that being vulnerable equaled being hurt and disappointed. She didn't think she could risk another heartache, and by the way she was feeling at that moment, she knew that Byron might cause her the kind of pain that would completely take her out.

Vicki felt the rapid beating of her heart, and no matter how many deep breathes she took, it would not slow down. Her hormones yelled at her to go back to him, to let him ravish her with his sweet kisses. Her stomach dropped, and a warm sensation spread across her gut at the mere thought of him touching her again. She squirmed in her seat, even more determined to block him out of her mind. Yes, she needed him, and worse, she wanted him. But one thing that dominated Vicki more than her wants and needs was her ability to remain in control. She started her vehicle and quickly drove away from Byron's loft without looking back once.

Vicki managed to avoid Byron for the most part over the next couple of weeks. She switched her office hours so that hers wouldn't collide with his and steered clear of her workspace as if it were a contagious disease. The few times she did bump into him, she shunned eye contact and kept her words short. She was grateful when the campus shut down the weekend before Thanksgiving because she desperately needed a break from both her students and Byron Bliss.

Vicki's dilemma about Thanksgiving remained, but she figured that she could prepare the dishes he had taught her and use cookbooks to make everything else. She wasn't completely secure with her culinary skills, but she had spent so much time trying to escape Byron's presence that she had not come up with a back-up plan for her holiday dinner. On Wednesday morning, she lay in her bed, trying to muster up the courage to begin cooking, knowing it would take her all day to make the majority of the menu. She would have stayed there forever, had her house phone not rung, forcing her up and out of the bed.

"Victoria!" a loud feminine voice shouted through the phone's ear piece.

"Yes, Aunt Mable," Vicki said sweetly, but was rolling her eyes simultaneously.

"What time is dinner tomorrow?"

"3 o'clock."

"Mm. Did you call everyone and tell them the time?"

"Yes, ma'am."

"Mm. Well, what you cookin'?"

"Same ol' things we always have during the holidays."

"Well this food better be right. Last year, your brother's wife's cooking gave me heartburn for a week. I told him that woman didn't know what she was doing. He should have never married her in the first place. What good is a woman who can't cook?"

Vicki held the phone silently, hoping her aunt's rant would end soon.

"You still in the bed? I hope not because you should be over there cooking already. You got a lot of mouths to feed tomorrow. Cousin Fred is coming, and he just had another baby. What's that like nine kids now? Him and that wife of his need to stop bringing all of these babies into the world when they ain't got no money to take care of them. And your Uncle Lou is coming with his two sons. You know them boys are as big as a house and will eat you out of yours. You need to get out of that bed! I'm sure glad them folks ain't coming over here, messing up my good furniture and putting me in the poorhouse. But you can afford it; you being a doctor and all."

Victoria let out an exhausted sigh. "Aunt Mable, you're right. I need to start cooking so I'll see you tomorrow at 3 PM."

"I'll be there at 1 o'clock," Aunt Mable responded sternly then hung up.

Vicki groaned at the thought of her overbearing family spending a day at her house. Normally, her twin sister Vivian would be around to help her cope, but this year Vivian and her husband were away, visiting his relatives in Georgia. She wished she could cancel the whole affair, but it was too late. She would have to suck up her bad attitude and deal with her family, like it or not.

She grabbed her white, terry cloth robe, slipped it on and headed downstairs to her kitchen. Vegetables, meats, fruits, breads, and spices cluttered her countertops and refrigerator. Feeling overwhelmed, she rubbed her forehead and closed her eyes, praying for the strength to complete the meal. A minute later, she opened her eyes, determined to survive the ordeal, starting with baking a pan of macaroni and cheese.

She pulled out a small notebook where she had written down the instructions Byron had given her about each dish. Feeling a bit more confident with the notes, she prepared the macaroni and cheese and put it in the oven to bake. Once it was baking, she decided to take a quick bath before starting on the other items. Inside the tub, she allowed herself to retreat to a place where Thanksgiving did not exist and her family treated her with understanding and acceptance.

By the time Vicki exited the safety of her bathroom over an hour later, she felt refreshed and relaxed. She turned on some smooth jazz as she lotioned her body and got dressed. She was pulling a pair of beige socks on her feet when she inhaled the aroma of something burning. She sniffed a few times then panicked when she realized that the macaroni and cheese was still baking in the oven.

"Oh no!" she shrieked.

She flew down the flight of stairs, dashed into the kitchen, and urgently opened the oven door. A small cloud of smoke poured out as she eyed her burned macaroni and cheese.

Frustrated, she yanked the pan out of the oven using oven mittens and tossed the inedible dish onto the granite countertop. Tears welled up in her eyes as she quickly realized that she wasn't capable of making a holiday meal for her entire family. She imagined them showing up the next day to a burned down kitchen and poorly cooked food. As much as she hated to say it, she needed Byron or she would be the laughing stock of her family. It had been a year since her brother's wife had fouled up the butter beans and her family still made unnecessary comments about it.

Crying and desperate, she picked up her cell phone and dialed Byron, hoping he would forgive her enough to rescue her.

"Hello?" he answered on the third ring. "Hel-lo?" he said again after she didn't reply immediately.

"Byron," she whispered.

"Vicki? Is that you? Are you okay?" Byron sounded alarmed.

Vicki sniffled. "It's me, but . . . I'm not okay."

"What happened? What's wrong?"

She closed her eyes, willing herself to tell the truth. "I . . . I need you. I can't do this on my own."

Byron paused, exhaled, and then said, "Text message me your address. I'm on my way."

Thirty minutes later, Vicki opened her front door and found Byron standing on the other side, smiling.

Feeling embarrassed, she lowered her eyes to the floor and opened the door wider so that he could enter. He stepped into the house, and she closed the door behind him, but before she could fully turn to face him, he moved in closer to her and placed a hungry kiss on her lips. Relieved that he still desired her, she wrapped her arms around him and returned the sultry kiss. He backed her body up against the door as he continued to explore her mouth with his. She wanted to get lost in the moment, but seconds later, he pulled away and she was instantly brought back to reality.

Byron scanned her briefly and laughed.

Confused, Vicki glared at him and said, "Why are you laughing at me?"

He took her left hand into his. "Because you're cute. And because you finally got real with me. It must have been pretty bad for you to let down your guard. So tell me, what happened?"

"I burned the macaroni and cheese," Vicki said, ashamed.

He laughed again "Some people like a little burn on their mac and cheese."

She shook her head. "No, it's really, really burned. No one will want it. Trust me."

"Okay, so have you made anything else?"

"No. I couldn't. I just called you."

"I see. Do you have any more cheese and macaroni shells?"

"No."

He kissed her forehead compassionately. "Listen, I need you to go to the store and get what we need to replace the macaroni and cheese. While you're doing that, I'll stay here and start cooking everything else."

She nodded and put on her coat to head to the store. Byron turned and began walking, searching for her kitchen. Before he was out of sight, Vicki called out to him. "Thanks for coming, Byron. I know I haven't been the easiest person to deal with, but I promise that I will be nicer from now on."

He spun around, grinned, and said. "I'm going to hold you to that."

Byron and Vicki spent the entire day and well into the night preparing the massive Thanksgiving meal, hoping it would be enough to satisfy her demanding relatives. Around four in the morning, Byron kissed her one last time on the cheek and returned to his own home. Vicki, exhausted from the endless hours of cooking and baking, collapsed in her bed and did not awake until noon on Thanksgiving.

Having overslept, she quickly showered and dressed and then began to warm the food for her family's arrival. Byron had helped her set-up the tables and chairs the day before, so all Vicki had to do was reheat the hot food and set it out on the buffet table. By ten after one, members of her family began to encroach about her house, surveying the meal as if they hadn't eaten in days. Instead of waiting until 3 o'clock, Vicki decided to allow people to eat as they came into the house, hoping it would reduce the amount of traffic in front of the buffet table and get her relatives out of her home faster. The new plan worked to her advantage, keeping her from having to fight with guest over trying to sneak pieces of chicken early.

"This is real, real nice," Aunt Mabel said, as she finished her second plate. "At least you can cook better than your brother's wife."

Katrina, Vicki's brother's wife, overheard the rude comment, folded her arms, and pouted in anger.

Vicki, understanding how hard it was to please her family, spoke in Katrina's defense. "You know, Aunt Mabel, it's a lot of work cooking for this many people, and you all don't even attempt to help with the food. I think you should show a little more appreciation. After all, it is Thanksgiving."

Aunt Mabel twisted her neck in indigence. "I am appreciative . . . that you know how to cook well enough not to kill me."

Vicki was beyond tired of her ill-mannered aunt and the rest of her greedy family. She no longer cared if they thought she could cook or even continued to view her as perfect. "Actually, I cannot take all of the credit. A friend of mine helped me with the food. To be honest, he prepared the majority of it," she stated.

Aunt Mabel sucked her teeth. "He? Who is he? You know I don't eat everybody's cooking."

Vicki smirked. "Well, today you ate his, two helpings of his cooking to be exact. Matter-of-fact, I think I will invite him over so that you can thank him for yourself."

Vicki stood up from where she was seated amongst her relatives and marched out of the dining area into the kitchen. She grabbed her cordless phone as she walked upstairs to gain some privacy. Sitting on her bed with her bedroom door closed, she dialed Byron's cell phone number, hoping he would answer.

"Hello," he answered in a groggy voice.

"Byron, it's me, Vicki. Did I wake you?"

"Yeah, but it's fine. What's the matter?"

"Nothing and everything. My family . . . they are driving me up the wall, but what else is new? Wait . . . why are you sleeping? Weren't you supposed to be having dinner with your family today?"

"I was supposed to, but I was up half the night helping a beautiful woman cook for her family, so I chose to sleep in and skip dinner. My family is eating dinner in Buffalo, and I don't feel like driving out there."

"Byron, I am so sorry! I didn't mean to cause you to miss having Thanksgiving with your family. Why didn't you tell me?"

"Vicki, it's okay. I have dinner with them all of the time. You needed me last night, and I wanted to be there for you. It was my choice; it's not your fault."

"I still feel bad. Why don't you come over and eat with us. There's still plenty of food left. Plus you can meet all of my annoying relatives that you spent half the night working to feed."

He hesitated then said, "Really? You're going to introduce me to your family? Are you sure?"

"Yes, I'm sure. Like I said before, I need you, but you'd better hurry up before I change my mind."

Byron chuckled. "Yes, ma'am. I'm on my way."

Vicki hung up the phone and smiled. For the first time in a long time, she appreciated the Department of Academic Affairs for their systematic changes, especially the one that led Dr. Byron Bliss into her office, life, and heart.

*For more of Victoria and Byron, check out Summer Secrets & Sins on page 131.

Winter Wonder of Love

By Kesha K. Redmon

It was an unusually blistering cold winter. The snowflakes fell big and fast. Tamar Landry couldn't believe her eyes. They were finally getting a white Christmas. Not that Memphis didn't ever receive any snow; it was just that it usually happened in the earlier part of the year.

Tamar eased onto the expressway toward her Cordova home. It was late, and she was tired and couldn't wait to curl up by her fireplace and read a good book. The thought alone brought a warm smile to her face. She had yet another late work day at St. Jude. She was a senior research scientist in the infectious disease department. She loved her job, but it was tedious and mentally draining. The hustle and bustle of the job is the reason she decided to take two weeks off and rejuvenate herself, so that she could come back invigorated and well rested and could figure out the best way to give cancer a swift kick in its metastasizing behind.

She decided to stop at the nearest Starbucks and get a venti hot chocolate and a marble pound cake. She knew the sweet combination would have her wired, but she had to have a treat. The weather was frightful, but she just couldn't help it. Her love for Starbucks could push her through any storm. This particular Starbucks was always pretty packed, but to her surprise, the place was empty when she walked through the door.

Relieved about not having to wait in line, she walked up to the counter to place her order. The cashier wearing a festive sweater asked, "How may I help you?"

"I would like a venti hot chocolate and a slice of marble pound cake," Tamar answered.

"That will be $5.85, the cashier replied, "and it will be right out."

"Well, somebody is going to be up all night."

Tamar twirled around to see a man who was the equivalent of a Greek god smirking at her. She assessed him from head to toe. He looked like he had just stepped off the pages of GQ magazine. Suit-Brioni, shoes-Kenneth Cole, watch-Movado, tie- silk, Burberry. She thought to herself, *"This man is very superficial."*

She looked into his hazel eyes and responded, "Well, it might look that way from the onset, but I'm sure I'll be just fine and asleep in not time." She turned back towards the counter just as the cashier was presenting her hot chocolate and cake. "Thank you and happy holidays," she told the cashier as she took her order and headed out the door, but not before getting another look at the Greek god. He gazed back at her, still wearing that same silly smirk on his face. She shook her head, walked out the door, and with the remote unlocked her car door. She placed the steaming hot chocolate into the cup holder and took a bite of the cake before closing her door and heading home.

She pulled into the garage of her four bedrooms, two and a half baths home. She grabbed her briefcase, purse, hot chocolate, and already half eaten cake and entered into her abode. Just as she put her belongings down, her phone rang. She rustled through her purse, pulled out the phone, and hit the answer button.

"Hello?" Tamar answered.

"Can you please put my info into your phone? We've been friends for all of these years, and you still don't recognize when I call. We're still friends, right?"

Tamar chuckled loudly. "Yes, Yolanda we're still friends. Your number isn't assigned because I like to hear you get shocked when I answer the phone. Girl, I knew it was you. How did you expect me to answer? 'What's up, chick?'"

Yolanda replied, "Yep, that's how we do it around these parts."

Tamar had to shake her head. She'd met Yolanda Crowley-Brown some years back at a singles' ministry seminar. They we're both hurting from past relationships and found solace in their growing friendship. Yolanda ended up meeting her husband there and now had three children--two girls and one boy—while Tamar was still waiting for her Mr. Right.

"Yolanda, what's up? How are my babies?"

"Girl, they are fine. Marcus is spoiling them to death. If I have to wrap one more gift and put it under the tree . . . Jesus be a fence."

"Stop it. You know you love the holidays. And you might as well get ready 'cause I'm bringing tons of more gifts."

Yolanda laughed. "Tamar that's fine as long as half of the tons are for me. I just called because Marcus and I are sponsoring a small group Bible class on Saturday night and wanted to know if you would like to come."

"You know that's Christmas Eve, Yolanda, right?"

"Of course, I know it's Christmas Eve. You don't have a man, and your parents are on vacay, so I know you're available. We don't want you to be over there crying your eyes out, singing that tired old Christmas song."

"What are you talking about, girl? You don't know if I have a man or not, and for goodness sake, what tired Christmas song are you referring to?" Tamar asked with an attitude.

"Look Missy, don't get snappy with me. I remember how lonely the holidays can be. You can come over and let the word of God fill you so you won't be over there singing that *What Do the Lonely Do*. I'll tell you what they do. They thank God in advance for the blessings He's about to give."

"Yolanda, seriously? I will not be singing that song. Yes, I do get lonely, and that's only because people like you are always reminding me that I am single. I'll come to your little Bible study, but you better tell that mannish Deacon Peters to keep his hands to himself. I ain't for all that foolishness."

"Chill out, he's not invited. Just a few close friends, and you better not shun Deacon Peters. At the rate you're going, you might have to marry that seventy year old man. I mean he gets his retirement, 401K, and social security. He might be what you need," Yolanda said as she burst into laughter. She howled so loudly that Tamar had to remove the phone from her ear.

"No, thanks. If there ever comes a day, and I see that there lies my fate in marrying him, I'll just as soon rapture up. Not gonna do it."

"That's why you don't have a man; you're too picky."

"I want somebody I can grow old with, not just some off-the-wall fleeting romance."

Yolanda sighed for her friend. "Just remember Tamar, the Bible says that it better to marry than to burn. Anyhoo, the study is on Saturday at 6 o'clock. Don't forget. I'll have pie and cobbler to feed that snack demon of yours, and don't forget to bring your Bible."

"Yada. Yada." Tamar teased. "I love you too." She hung up the phone and made her way to her upstairs suite. The holidays were here and almost gone, and she would spend another year alone. She hated the fact that she didn't have anyone to spend the holidays with. She wiped her make-up from her face and exfoliated her skin. Next, she ran a bubble bath in her Jacuzzi tub and placed herself into the middle of it. The combination of the heat and the jet was like a massage to her aching and stressed muscles. She thought back to the conversation she'd had with Yolanda. She made some very good points. As far as Tamar was concerned, her relationship status was in God's hands now.

Friday, Tamar got up early so she could do some last minute shopping. It's funny how she didn't mind the hustle and bustle of the shopping crowds during the holidays, but, any other time, it drove her insane. She entered the Toys R Us/Babies R Us combo store and grabbed a shopping cart. She planned on doing some major damage. Yolanda's kids ranged in ages from fifteen months to six. Tamar loved those kids, and they loved her in return. They affectionately called her "Tee-Tee Tay-Tay." She made sure they knew how much she loved them by never letting a moment go by when she wasn't spoiling them.

She perused the toy aisles with the little one in mind first. She couldn't believe how many educational/learning type toys were on the market for toddlers. Tamar stood in amazement. Now, she knew why the kids at St. Jude were so smart. As she reached for a learning laptop, a hand blocked her movement. "Not that one." She turned around to see who the rude culprit was, and it was none other than Mr. Star "Mega" Bucks himself.

"Do you come here often?" Tamar asked snidely.

"Actually, I do not. How about yourself?"

Tamar couldn't help but roll her eyes. "Well, actually I do."

"That's funny," the ever always well-dressed stranger retorted.

"What's funny?" Tamar asked while starring him directly in the eyes, waiting to seize the moment when she could go off on this handsome stranger.

"You don't strike me as the motherly type."

That was her moment, the time for her to put her neck roll into action. She prepped for it, took a deep breath, and her mouth fell open in shock. The stranger placed his pointer under the base of her chin and closed her mouth for her. Tamar was livid, and she let her anger boil to the top.

"Who do you think you are?" Tamar asked angrily.

He extended his right hand and made a formal introduction. "I am Washington Parker. All my friends call me Wash, but you can call me Washington."

"Oh, I know *exactly* what to call you, you piece of . . ." Tamar stopped abruptly when she heard the giggle. She looked down to see the most precious little angel who had covered her ears with her hands.

"You're about to be naughty, and Santa is not going to like that at all," she scolded Tamar.

Tamar bowed down to the child's level and grabbed her two ponytails dangling from each side and fluffed them. "You are absolutely right. I don't want to end up on Santa's naughty list along with someone else," she remarked as she turned in the direction of Mr. Washington Parker, giving him an evil stare all the while.

"Oooh. Santa saw that too," the little girl cooed pointing at Tamar.

Tamar had to laugh at the little girl. She was just as adorable as she could be. "What's your name?" Tamar asked lovingly.

"My name is Alyssa Nicole Parker. You can call me Alyssa Nicole Parker," the little girl answered with an outstretched right hand.

"Well," said Tamar, "Ms. Alyssa Nicole Parker, how old are you?"

"I'm four."

"You are the brightest four year old I've ever seen," Tamar complimented.

"Thanks," she replied as she hid behind Washington's designer trousers.

"It was a pleasure seeing you again, Washington, although we simply must stop meeting this way."

"Oh, don't be a party-pooper. I know the sight of me brightens your day."

"You could only wish." Tamar grabbed a hold to her shopping cart and winked at the little princess. She decided that Toys R Us wasn't the place for her. Target was looking mighty good, but she would need to go now while Washington was here. She didn't want to have another run in him.

Tamar could not believe Christmas was one day away. Her 6 feet tall white Christmas tree adorned with silver, red, and green ornaments was simply beautiful and breathtaking. She couldn't help but stare as she made her way down the stairs from her bedroom. It was definitely a focal point of the living room. Her thoughts were interrupted by the ringing of her home phone. She checked the caller ID before answering.

"Hi, Mom."

"Oh hello, my darling. How are you this Christmas Eve morning?"

"I'm great. How are you and Dad?"

"We are having an absolutely wonderful time. Wish you were here."

"No you don't, Mom," Tamar teased. She knew that her parents were having the time of their lives in the Caribbean.

"Have you found me a son-in-law yet? I keep telling you, don't wait too late to start having babies. You're gonna be just like that cow, Lisa Faye. She waited until she was thirty-six to have a baby and now she can't lose the weight to save her life. You're thirty-two. You know the body doesn't do well with the metabolic process once you're in your mid thirties. So, you best get started."

Tamar was very used to the old maid references and ramblings of her mother. She just couldn't believe she called Lisa Faye a cow. That poor woman had a hard time conceiving. She was just happy that Lisa was finally able to have a child.

"Mother, Lisa is happy with an adorable baby boy. I'm sure gaining a few pounds was well worth the sacrifice for becoming a mother. Besides, you can hardly tell."

"You know good and well that girl is as big as a palace."

Tamar needed to change the subject quickly before this whole situation went south.

"So, Mom, where's Dad?"

"He's right here. Hold on a second."

Tamar could hear her mother waking her father. *They must still be in the hotel*, she thought.

"Baby girl, how are you?"

"I'm well, Father. How are you?" Tamar asked.

"Your mother and I are having an awfully good time. I'm just sad that we won't be together for Christmas this year."

"It's quite okay, Dad. Yolanda has invited me over, so I won't be alone."

"Good. Glad to hear that. Your mother and I should be home for the New Year. We'll have a nice time together then."

"Okay, sounds great, Dad. Enjoy yourselves."

"We will, sweetie. Talk to you later."

"You too." Tamar hung up the phone feeling a little bit lonely and nostalgic with her parents being away for the holidays.

Her parents always made sure they were home for the holidays, mostly because they didn't want to leave Tamar alone. This year they got a fabulous deal on a holiday vacation in the Caribbean, and her parents, Drake and Lorraine Landry, could not pass on the deal to celebrate their thirty-third wedding anniversary.

Tamar loved the fact that her parents were still together and going strong. She always got a little sink in her heart when it came down to her present relationship status as compared to that of her parents.

Tamar was just about to make breakfast when the phone rang again.

"Hello, Yolanda."

"Yes! Yolanda screamed emphatically. "That's how I want you to always answer from this point on.

"O . . . K . . ." Tamar replied. "What's going on?"

"Well, there's been a change of plans."

"Oh-uh. What does that mean exactly?" Tamar questioned.

"It means that the Bible study has turned into a Christmas Eve party. Marcus thought that since we were going to be at church Sunday, Bible study would be overkill. So, we've decided just to have a little party instead.

"So, what's the big deal then?"

"The big deal is I have no party food. I need you to go shopping with me and help me prepare some of this food. It has to be on point because he's inviting big wigs, and he wants to make a good impression. As if I didn't already have enough to do."

"Calm down. I'm here for you girl. It's 9:00 AM now. Let me get dressed, and we can meet up at the market."

"Don't forget to bring clothes Tamar. The party is still at six. We have a lot to do and you won't have time to go back home."

"Okay, Yolanda. I'll meet you at the market at eleven." Tamar hung up the phone and took a deep sigh. She knew that her friend was stressed, and being the friend that she was, she would be right there to help her friend.

Tamar pulled up to the market at 10:58 AM, bright-eyed and bushy tailed. She did a quick scan of the parking lot in search of Yolanda's Nissan Quest. Just as she was about to dial her up on the phone, Yolanda tapped her window. Tamar opened the door and got out of her car to greet her friend with a hug "Hey, Yolanda."

"Hey, Tamar. I'm sorry to bother you like this, but I really need your help."

"No problem. That's what friends are for. You know I have your back, and I don't mind one iota."

"Great. Let's get started. I brought coupons," Yolanda squealed as she waved her prized coupon binder.

Tamar sighed because she knew this could become very ugly. Yolanda had recently begun clipping coupons and like everything she took an interest in, she worked it to her advantage which meant the disadvantage was left for everyone else. The ladies entered the market, and Yolanda quickly grabbed a cart.

Tamar and Yolanda walked down the aisles of the supermarket selecting various meats, cheeses, and breads. They halted at the beverage aisle.

"Tamar," Yolanda voice, "I think we should make some ghetto punch."

"Ghetto punch? What in the world is that?" Tamar questioned.

"Girl, I forget, you were born into privilege."

"Yolanda, growing up in a middle class family is hardly privileged."

"So you think. My parents struggled just to feed all five of us. If not for the grace of God, I don't know how we would have made it."

"But for the grace of God is how we all made it, Yolanda," Tamar chimed in. "I know times were hard back then. We all made it and for the better. That's all that matters. So, who's going to be in attendance at this fabulous soiree?' Tamar asked quickly changing the subject.

"Just a lot of Marcus' pals and work partners, along with people whom he is trying to go into business with."

"Sounds like some serious heavy hitters. We might want to reconsider this ghetto punch idea," Tamar chuckled.

Yolanda rolled her eyes deeply at her friend. "Whatever. We're having ghetto punch. Besides, I need something to be able to put my gin in."

"Really! Really? You're planning on getting drunk at your husband's business party?"

"I'm not going to get drunk. It will help me calm my nerves. Trust me, these people can be a little uptight and boring, and the kids need something to drink on as well."

"Somehow, I don't think having the kids at the party is a good idea."

"Marcus and I discussed that, and he said that everybody thought it would be cool to bring the kids along so that they can get to know each other."

"Okay. I get that. I just don't get the alcohol, but it's your party, and you can get lit if you want."

Yolanda led Tamar to the Kool-Aid aisle and picked up different packets of Kool-Aid. They then added sugar, sherbet, canned orange juice, 7-UP to their supply lost for their punch recipe.

When they got to the checkout, Yolanda did her extreme couponing thing as Tamar stood in shock. The total rang up to $529.16. After Yolanda had the cashier enter in all her coupons, her total came down to $71.80.

"Wow!" Tamar gushed, "You saved a whole lot of money."

"I know, right? This is so much fun. Marcus always gives me a budget to work with. I work with it all right. I save that extra money, divide it by three, and put it in the children's' accounts. I want them to go to college, and every extra penny I save will help. You'll understand when you start pumping babies out."

"I just want to know why I have to be pumping babies out. Your kids are going to be so grateful to you for that. Most parents don't worry about their kids' education until it's too late."

"So I hear, Tamar. Our kids are going to grow up different. We're going to make sure they are prepared and well educated. We're going to make sure they participate in everything that can make them better. We just need you to get married and start having babies. I won't to experience all this with you. So, get to cracking."

Tamar laughed. "Yolanda, I'm trying really hard. I never thought it would be so difficult for me to find someone to share my life with. I meet men all the time. They just never seem to work out, and I don't know exactly why."

"I can tell you why, ma'am. You are emotionally unavailable to the men you meet. You put work on such high priority that you never make time for social relationships. Then when the relationship doesn't work, you take it out on every man your meet from that point. You need to get your life right."

"Well, thank you, Tamar Braxton, for the life coaching skills," Tamar said rolling her eyes at her friend. "I'm not going to spend the rest of my life worrying about whether or not I'll have a man in my life. When the time comes, if being in a relationship is meant for me then everything will work itself out."

The ladies arrived at Yolanda's and began preparing the food for the party. Tamar was surprised to find out that Yolanda had also already pre-made some of Christmas dinner as well. Tamar loved the holidays, and being with Yolanda and her family made them special. The ladies worked swiftly, for it was 2:30 and they had to also get ready.

As they were putting their finishing touches on the sandwiches, Marcus, Yolanda's husband, walked in. He glowed when he saw his wife's best friend. He loved Tamar like a sister and he told her so often. "Tamar, how are you?" Marcus asked as he kissed his wife and hugged his friend.

Tamar had to stand on her tip-toes to embrace Marcus. "I'm great Marcus. How are you?"

"I'm well. Can't complain," Marcus replied. "Just bringing the kids back from seeing Santa.

As if on cue, the kids sauntered in with delight upon seeing their aunt. "Tee-Tee Tay Tay," the children screamed as they each waited to receive a hug from Tamar. Tamar's heart melted as she felt the love radiating from the little ones to herself. She picked up fifteen month old Aleena and nuzzled her neck. The toddler squealed in delight. "Tay-Tay," she beckoned with her arms outstretched to give Tamar another hug. Not to be outdone, three-year-old Jarvis grabbed her pants leg and wrapped himself around her leg for dear life, while six-year-old Graced smiled.

"Tee-Tee Tay Tay, my new friend Nikki is coming over today and we're gonna have so much fun. I can't wait. It's going to be the best day of my life," Grace informed Tamar of the coming event.

"Well, it's good your friend is coming over Grace. I know you're going to have a wonderful time together."

"Me too," Jarvis said trying not to be left out."

"You too, Jarvis," Tamar confirmed as she grabbed his hand and headed toward the upstairs bedroom. Tamar turned towards Marcus and Yolanda. "We're going to get dressed. See you guys at show time."

The party was in full swing by the time Tamar made her grand entrance with the kids. They were so excited; Jarvis and Grace bounced down the stairs. She held Grace in her arms as she tried to balance on the six inch stilettos and the long Commes des Garcon sheath. It was 7 o'clock and she could already tell that the party was a huge success. Marcus was working the room effortlessly, greeting and entertaining his guests. She looked for Yolanda only to find her in a corner sipping her ghetto punch.

"Uh-oh," Tamar said as she ran to her friend to rescue her from making a scene. She snatched the cup from Yolanda's hand.

"Hey, I was drinking that!" Yolanda exclaimed.

Tamar responded by giving her Aleena. Yolanda rebutted by putting Aleena down and snatching her cup back from Tamar.

"I know you didn't just take my cup," Yolanda said.

"I was trying to save you from yourself. You don't want to end up embarrassing Marcus later on tonight after you've had too many of these, and who puts their child down in exchange for liquor? Tamar fussed.

"Who gives a small child to someone who is indulging?" Yolanda retorted.

Aleena responded by leaving the two in the midst of their debate. Just as the two were about to go into a deeper conversation, they were interrupted by Marcus' voice.

"Ladies, Ladies. Tamar I have someone I want you to meet."

Tamar stopped mid-sentence. She smelled him before she saw him. As she spun around, it was none other than Mr. Washington Parker. He put a silly smirk on his face when he saw Tamar's expression.

"Wash," Marcus introduced, "I would like you to meet Tamar Landry, and you already know my wife."

Tamar rolled her eyes. This little action was not missed by Marcus or Yolanda.

Yolanda extended her hand, "Glad you could make it, Wash."

Grace came bouncing through the great room. "Mommy, Mommy, look— it's Nikki. She's finally here."

"Hi, Nikki. Glad you could come too." Nikki responded by giving her the sheepish grin that Tamar had become familiar with.

Nikki looked up and caught sight of Tamar and waived. Tamar returned the gesture in kind. "Hi, Alyssa Nicole Parker."

"I don't know your name. What's your name?" Alyssa asked.

"That's my Tee-Tee Tay Tay," Grace answered before Tamar could even part her lips.

"I'm Tamar," Tamar said to the little girl as she grabbed a ponytail. "Nice to see you again."

"You two know each other?" Marcus asked, looking puzzled from Tamar to Wash.

"Unofficially" Wash explained. "We've had a couple of run-ins."

"More like your friend here is a stalker," Tamar told Marcus as she gave her opinion about the matter.

Tamar and Wash exchange meaningful banter and playful body language as Yolanda sat back watching.

Tamar's insinuation of the word stalker had Wash in stitches.

"Stalker? Please. I am a man of many means and excellent, well-defined talents, and I can guarantee you that stalking is not one. You should consider yourself blessed that you can be in the presence of such class as myself."

Tamar watched as Marcus grabbed the drink from Yolanda and took a sip. His palate was not easily fooled, and he raised an eyebrow as if to Yolanda to let her know.

Tamar hissed as she placed her hands on her hips, "I cannot fathom from what dark deep pit you have escaped from; but you Wash are…"

"It's Washington to you."

That did it. She'd had enough. She grabbed the already passed around drink from Marcus' hand and threw it in Washington's face. Yolanda covered her mouth while Marcus smiled from ear to ear. The red punch ran down Washington's flawless caramel skin into what Tamar could tell was a very expensive Italian suit.

She suddenly felt embarrassed at her actions and looked around to see who was watching. Fortunately, it seemed everyone else had spiked their ghetto punch as well because they had created a dance floor and seemed to be having an awfully good time. Tamar sighed in relief. She'd had altercations with men before, but none of them got her riled up like Washington. As soon as she thought she was safe, she looked down to see five sets of eyes on her. Apparently, Jarvis had made a friend at the party and they seemed to be hanging tough.

Alyssa looked at Tamar as the tears begin to stream from her eyes. "You're mean. Santa is not going to come to your house tonight. Why are you bullying my daddy?"

Tamar's heart broke into pieces, and it showed on her face. She could not believe she had allowed herself to stoop so low, especially, in front of children.

"I'm so sorry, Alyssa. I didn't mean to. I'm real clumsy sometimes, and it was an accident."

Grace looked at Tamar sideways, and Marcus was in stitches. It seemed he could no longer hold his emotions. All the laughter he had maintained spewed out into a hearty bellow. Yolanda appeared unsure of what to do as she stood frozen in time.

Finally Marcus spoke, "Grace, take Alyssa to your room and play for a minute. I'll be up to check on you guys, okay?" he said, looking from one little girl to the next.

Both of the little girls nodded and headed upstairs along with the rest of the group—except for a straggler— Aleena. Aleena was now raising her leg to kick Wash. Yolanda quickly grabbed the child before she could inflict more embarrassment on her guest.

"I see you've decided to let your true colors shine through," Wash told Tamar while giving her an under-eyed glare."

"I am so sick of your little cocky, arrogant attitude," Tamar responded. "I've had quite enough of you, sir. You go way too far. You don't know me at all." Tamar stormed towards upstairs. She heard Marcus call her name; but she refused to have any conversation in the presence of Mr. High and Mighty.

It was 10 o'clock before Tamar made her way back downstairs. Yolanda had rounded up all the kids to be ushered to their respective parents. It had taken Tamar nearly an hour to calm Nikki down, a situation that only added to her disappointment in herself.

When she made it downstairs, she saw Marcus and Wash cleaning up. She couldn't help it. She had to smirk. Wash had been reduced to a pair of jeans and a pullover. She secretly did a little happy dance in her head. When he turned around, the celebration quickly ended. He looked fabulous. She could have thrown up. She wanted to see him reduced—his attitude and humility—by desecrating the one thing she thought mattered to him: his image. All she did was confirm what he already knew—he was all that.

Their eyes made contact. He stood firm. She cracked. She could've kicked herself for being so weak. She walked towards him to make her amends.

"Look, Wash… I mean Washington, I want to apologize for my behavior earlier. I was completely out of line, especially in front of the children. Alyssa is sleeping. She was very excited for Santa. I'm sure she can't wait to tell him how I don't deserve a gift.

Marcus chuckled, "Where's Yolanda?"

"She fell asleep in Grace's room."

"Drunk, no doubt?" Marcus asked Tamar.

She was careful not to give anything away from her facial expressions. He raised his eyebrows, kissed her on the cheek, and went upstairs. Wash remained quiet, taking the trash out to the curb, while Tamar stood looking like a nut in the middle of the floor. She sighed deeply and grabbed her purse and keys form behind the sofa. As she prepared to leave, she was interrupted by Marcus.

"Where do you think you're going?"

"Home," Tamar answered. "I think I've done enough damage for one night." She cut a glance to Wash who was now sitting outside in a chair in the opened garage, drinking a soda and starring at the night.

"You have clothes here, so you might as well stay," Marcus suggested while looking out to see what Tamar was gazing intently at. "That man right there is one of the realest dudes I know. He's just in need of some real love right now. His faith has been tested, and he's going through a lot right now. He's had a pretty hard year. Just cut him some slack for now, please?"

Tamar only responded to Marcus with a head nod. She was curious to know how someone who needed love could be so cold and calculating. She spent the next ten minutes watching him from the window as this back heaved up and down.

Tamar awoke the next morning to laughter and the smell of maple syrup. Immediately, her mouth begin salivate. She forced herself out of the bed and headed down the hall to the bathroom. She balked at the sight before her. Her hair was a mess. She began to clean up and pull her hair up into the shower cap. She had to take a shower before she could do anything with her hair.

When Tamar got out of the shower, she wasn't at all surprised to see a beautiful robe hanging on the back of the door. She put the robe on and headed downstairs. She was shocked, however, by the sight before her. Wash was flipping pancakes for the kids, and they were tickled to death. She smiled at the softer, lighter side of this seemingly dark character.

"Morning," Tamar greeted everyone. "Merry Christmas."

The kids ran up to her, giving big hugs and wet kisses. "Merry Christmas, Tee-Tee Tay Tay," they answered in unison.

Tamar blushed as she looked up to see Alyssa looking intently at them. Tamar extended her hand towards the child. "Aren't you going to give me a hug, Alyssa?" The little girl perked up and ran into her arms. Tamar squeezed all four children tightly as they giggled and squirmed in her arms.

"Okay, that's enough, you guys. Let's finish eating. We have to go to services this morning, and I know you want to open some of your presents."

The kids rushed back to the table and began to devour the food.

"Merry Christmas, everyone," Tamar started again.

Marcus and Yolanda returned the sentiment while Wash opted instead to place a plate of pancakes and some sausage in front of her. She nodded her head and ate. There was small talk here and there, but no words were exchanged between the two.

The children proceeded to opening their gifts. Grace's scream could've have wakened wolves in Siberia. "Thanks, Tee-Tee Tay Tay. I've wanted one of these my whole life," she said as ran around the room with her new iPad.

"An iPad. Really? An iPad?" Marcus asked quizzically.

"Well, I bought it as an educational tool. I preloaded it with learning apps and . . ."

Yolanda shorted her statement, "There had better be some diamonds under that tree for me. I know that if you've bought an expensive gift for a child, I best be getting some gems."

Tamar brushed Yolanda off. "Whatever. That gift under the tree with your name on it is the gift you're getting. Deal with it."

Jarvis opened his gift to reveal a train set, while Aleena uncovered a Baby Alive doll.

"Tell me that thing doesn't pee," Yolanda demanded.

"Naw. She poops." Tamar burst into laughter.

"You better pray while we're at church. Aleena isn't even out of diapers yet, and you're going to bring me something else to change. I can't wait until you start having babies."

Grace brought Marcus' gift and his face lit-up brighter than the Christmas tree. "Season tickets to the Grizzlies games. Yes! Oh wait . . . Are these floor seats?"

"I got a discount through St. Jude," Tamar replied.

Yolanda was fuming. She got up and went to the tree. Under the tree was a huge box with her name on it. She opened the box and was taken aback. Inside held the most elegant red and black color blocked suit that she'd ever seen. And the end all to be all was lying next to it: red bottoms. Yolanda spoke no words as tears formed in the corner of her eyes. Marcus looked on stunned while Wash's face feigned in difference.

"Thank you, Tamar."

"You're welcome Yolanda, Merry Christmas."

Tamar took a side glance at Nikki who had opened her gifts from Marcus and Yolanda and her father. She had at her side clothes, an American Girl doll, and a Kurio kid's tablet, but, she looked so sad. Tamar went to the child and kneeled beside her.

"Did you open the gift I bought you?" Tamar asked.

Nikki looked up at Tamar quizzically and shook her head no. Tamar found the gift and placed it in the child's hand. The box was almost bigger than she was. Nikki tore through the wrapping and opened the box. Tamar heard the gasp. She pulled from the box a red beaded quilted dress with a black cummerbund and a long sleeved bolero to match. There was also a gold necklace with a crown pendant that said PRINCESS.

"Thank you so much. It's beautiful." Nikki said as she held the dress up to her frame.

"You are so very welcome." Tamar tapped the little girl's nose and nuzzled her neck. "Let's go get ready for church."

Tamar grabbed the little girl's things while Nikki exclaimed to her dad, "I'm a princess." Wash and Marcus laughed at her antics and confirmed what she already knew. When Tamar stood she was face to face with Wash, but he said no words. He didn't have to; his eyes said it all.

Tamar was relieved that everything had worked out. Nikki was spinning around watching herself in the floor length mirror. The dress was so beautiful on her it really did make her look like a princess. Tamar had put her up in a bun and tied red and black ribbons on it that she borrowed from Grace. She smiled at the sight of the happy child.

The night prior, she didn't know how to fix the mess she had created. Nikki was so upset. She'd had to make decisions and make them fast. The iPad that was originally for Yolanda became Grace's. The dress that Nikki now wore was meant for Grace, and the suit and shoes she'd bought for herself became Yolanda's. She was thanking

God they all wore the same sizes. *The Lord does work in mysterious ways.* She now wore a green sweater dress and brown 5 inch Pucci boots. She accented her look with gold jewelry and a side pony. It was now 10 o'clock. If they didn't leave soon, they wouldn't get any good seats.

Tamar brought Nikki down stairs and waited for the others. Everyone looked their Sunday best. Wash had on a Brooks Brother suit that was everything it should be on his well-built frame. He gave Tamar a slight smile as he took his daughter from her arms.

"All right, let's get going," Marcus said as he checked out everyone for readiness.

"I wanna ride with Tee-Tee Tay Tay," Nikki begged.

Wash reluctantly put her down, led her to Tamar's car and strapped her in.

"Love you," he said, giving Nikki a kiss on her forehead.

"Love you more, Daddy."

Tamar smiled as she watched the exchange from her rear view mirror. Wash tapped on the passenger window and Tamar pressed the button to roll the window down.

"Thank you," Wash said as he placed his hands in his pockets and gently tilted his head down as those two words were the hardest he ever had to utter. Tamar returned the courtesy with a smile.

Church was filling up rather quickly. Marcus led the group down close to the front so the kids would be able to see the dramas. No sooner than they had sat down than they were approached by none other than Deacon Peters himself. Tamar froze as he came closer and pretended like he was greeting her with a kiss, except he was using his tongue. Yolanda side glanced Marcus, and Wash looked on in disgust as Tamar squirmed to get away.

Wash broke up the unceremonious greeting by extending his right hand to the deacon and placing his left arm around Tamar. "Washington Parker."

Deacon Peters looked taken aback as he grabbed Wash's hand for a firm handshake. Tamar's body relaxed a little. Marcus raised an eyebrow, and Yolanda leaned forward for a better view.

The deacon wasted no time in returning the formal introduction, "Deacon Ernest Peters. Nice to meet you. You're new," Deacon Peters stated, but, it came out more like a question.

Wash chuckled, "I've been around."

Deacon Peters withdrew and took a step back. He knew when he had been bested, and there was no way he could ever compete on the same level with Wash.

Wash retracted his arm. Marcus gave a fist pump, Nikki climbed onto Tamar's lap, and Yolanda started praying like never before.

The church service was awesome. The choir had been spectacular. The kids enjoyed themselves so much they had bounced and clapped along with the choir. They were still singing "What a Wonderful Child" long after the song had ended.

Tamar was perplexed as to Washington Parker. The pastor had preached the sermon, "A New Light, A New Hope." Washington seemed torn the whole service. She wanted answers, and she decided she would ask.

Later, she and Yolanda were putting out dinner. They had been joined by Marcus' and Yolanda's parents who were entertaining the children with Christmas songs. Tamar took the undisturbed moment to get answers. "Yolanda, what's Wash's story?"

Yolanda turned to look at Wash who was watching the game. "I don't know the whole story. Just bits and pieces. He's had a really hard couple of years. He's wife lost her battle with cancer. Her family is angry because they feel like he didn't do enough to keep her here, so he moved from Atlanta. He's a big time attorney, you know.

"Wow. That would explain the over confident-cockiness."

Yolanda looked at Tamar and smiled.

"What?" Tamar asked.

"Nothing," Yolanda replied. "Let's eat."

At dinner, Wash's whole attitude towards Tamar had changed as well as had hers. The two even participated in playful banter that didn't appear to be lost on Yolanda.

"So, Wash did you enjoy the service?" Yolanda asked.

"Yolanda, services were totally amazing, just like this wonderful meal. I want to thank you guys for everything you've done for us."

"No problem," Marcus chimed in. "You're like a brother to me. I could never turn my back on you, and don't you forget it."

"Thanks, man. It's just been hard. My mom does her best, but she should never have to be a mother again. She's a grandmother, and I didn't want her to have that responsibility."

"What about Jamillah's parents? Yolanda asked.

"My wife's parents are heartbroken. Jamillah's death left them inconsolable. Alyssa's presence makes it worst, I think. They send gifts, visit, and send for her, but, it's too much sometimes. I understand. It's just that I . . ."

"Need help," Tamar finished his sentence.

Wash looked up and nodded his confirmation.

"May I ask what did she pass from?" Tamar questioned.

Wash looked at Alyssa as she was playing a board game with the other kids. "She had breast cancer. She found out while she was three months pregnant with Alyssa. She refused chemo and couldn't beat it afterwards. It was out of control. She told me she had no regrets because she had been given Alyssa.

"I'm so sorry for your loss." Tamar gave her condolences as she wiped tears with her dinner napkins. "How has Alyssa been doing?"

"She has nightmares, and she misses her mom terribly; but, I think she's faring well. Thank you for being so nice to her. She really likes you."

"That's because I'm a likable person. Well, at least to some people."

Yolanda and Marcus as well as their parents laughed at the sly comment meant for Wash.

Wash laughed. "You're just a little too uptight."

"You know, Tamar, we haven't given you are gift," Yolanda intervened before the conversation between Tamar and Wash went south.

Tamar clapped her hands. "Oh goodie! What did you get me?"

Marcus got up from the table and brought her the most beautiful royal blue box tied with a white ribbon. Yolanda gushed at seeing her friend go wide eyed at the presence of the box.

It's so beautiful, y'all!" Tamar commented as she proceeded to open the box. Her mouth fell open at the sight of its contents.

Inside was a treasure trove of books, all her favorite. She was tickled at how many fit into the box. She counted ten. She paused as there was an envelope underneath. She opened the envelope and knew immediately from whence it came. Because Marcus' and Yolanda's parents were in attendance, she'd have to wait to cut the fool.

"Thanks you guys," Tamar said to Yolanda and Marcus, "This is a wonderful gift."

Yolanda gave Tamar a little smirk. "You're absolutely welcome. We just wanted you to know how much we care about you," she winked.

Tamar responded by rolling her eyes as hard as she could. Yolanda responded in kind by getting up, grabbing another envelope, and handing it to Wash. Wash peered at the envelope, then looked at Marcus who pointed to Yolanda slyly, and sat down at the kitchen bar. Tamar's interest piqued, and it showed when she raised an eyebrow.

Tamar watched as Wash opened the envelope and did a double take. She saw the recognition in his face that said he knew Yolanda was behind the envelope giving. After all, it was part of her chemical makeup to do something so sneaky and secretive. "Gee, thanks guys. This sure will come in handy," he said nonchalantly.

Tamar giggled uncontrollably as Marcus shoved her playfully. Wash placed the envelope in the inside of his suit pocket. "I want to thank you guys for being the consummate hosts that you always are. You've made this holiday more than memorable." With that being said, Wash gave the group hugs. His hug to Tamar was quick and unaffectionate. He called for Alyssa to come, but she stopped directly in front of Tamar. Tamar leaned in to give the child the warmest hug she could muster. Alyssa held on, and then she whispered something into Tamar's ear.

It was New Year's Eve and Tamar had spent the days in between reading. Yolanda had done really well with her selection of books. Tamar was about to take a break and watch TV. When her phone rang, she picked it up without checking the caller ID.

"Hello," she answered.

"Hello, a deep sultry voice replied, "Tamar, this is Wash."

She immediately perked up. She hadn't heard a thing about or from him since Christmas. This call was definitely a surprise.

"I hope it's okay that I'm calling you. Yolanda gave me your number. I hope you don't mind."

"That's fine Wash . . . ington. How can I help you?"

"I'm calling because as you know, tonight is New Year's Eve, and there is a Zoo Snooze at the zoo and Alyssa has been begging me to ask you to come. There will be vendors as well as musical entertainment. So, do you want to ring in the New Year with Alyssa?"

Tamar sat quietly for a moment. Interestingly enough, Yolanda spoke of this same event a few days ago. "Well, if Ms. Alyssa Nicole Parker requests my presence, who am I not to oblige?"

Wash stammered, "Uh, oh...okay. I'll let her know when she wakes up from her nap. She will be thrilled. Thanks for agreeing to come."

"No problem," Tamar stated, "What time does the event begin?"

"It starts at 5:00 P.M. They'll have different acts performing. I don't intend to stay all night because I don't want her in the crowds, and I think she's too young. So, I'm planning to leave around seven or eight."

"Okay, sure Wash."

"I'll pick you up around 4:00 P.M. Will that be okay?"

Tamar looked at the clock; it was now 12:00 noon. "I'll be ready. Would you like me to meet you there?"

"No, we can come pick you up. What's the address?"

Tamar hesitantly spouted off her address to Wash.

"See you soon," Wash said and hung up the phone."

Tamar stood by her floor length mirror assessing her look and decided on a low key look. She wore jeans, a sweater, and paired them with her black Uggs. She needed to be warm if she were going to be outside. All the snow had melted, but it was still pretty cold outside, and she couldn't afford to get sick. That's the very reason she chose her black newsboy cap to wear on her head.

She made her way downstairs just as the bell rang. When she opened it, Alyssa ran straight into her arms. Tamar picked her up and spun her around. Alyssa threw her head back in laughter. They were having so much fun that Wash had to made his presence known by clearing his throat.

Tamar acknowledged his action, "Hey, Washington. Let me just grab my coat and purse, and we can be on our way."

The ride in the Escalade was like smooth sailing. Wash had the radio on Sirius' Kids Place Live, and Alyssa sang the entire way. Tamar and Wash engaged in conversation, but keep it light all the way. The traffic became heavy as they approached their destination. Wash had to drive around the parking lot to find the perfect spot. Alyssa didn't want to walk and started complaining. Wash ignored her, and she began to pout to show her disapproval. Tamar thought she looked so cute with her lip poked out, so she picked the child up.

"Okay, when you get tired and your back starts to hurt, don't ask me for help," Wash told Tamar.

"She's not even that heavy." Tamar chastised Wash as she cradled the child in her arms.

They walked until they arrived at the ticket gate. Alyssa jumped from Tamar's arms to collect all the trinkets she saw being given away. Tamar and Wash followed behind. Wash found a spot that was nestled on the outskirts of the event, but was still close enough to see all the activity.

"She's having way too much fun," Tamar commented to Wash as she watched Alyssa bounced around singing and dancing.

"She's a ball of energy and a handful," Wash responded.

With Tamar toting Alyssa, three walked around, viewing all the animals and their activities. Tamar almost ran off, nearly dropping Alyssa in the process, when she saw the monkey swinging from the tree overhead. Wash caught her just in the nick of time.

She gasped, "I can't believe they let those wild things wander around aimlessly. Someone could get hurt."

"They're completely harmless, I guess." Wash chuckled. "Surely, they wouldn't let them loose if they were dangerous."

"I don't care how harmless the zoo thinks they are. I've seen enough of *When Animals Go Wild* to know that they could be potentially dangerous."

At first, Tamar froze as Wash engulfed her in a sweet, warm, and delicate embrace, but her body went from rigid to relaxed in a matter of seconds. It felt like heaven, and her being felt free. But her escape was interrupted by Alyssa's voice.

"Let's go. More to see. More to do."

Tamar felt Wash's embrace leave, and he guided them further along the path to more animals and more freebies for Alyssa.

They ventured upon the makeshift bleachers that faced the stage for the entertainment. Tamar smiled as she watched all the kids dancing, singing and running around. She felt a little pang of guilt that the kids of St. Jude would have to spend their holiday cooped up inside a hospital. She was praying that one day cancer would be as treatable as the common cold. She brought her mind back to the event in front of her and found herself dancing and enjoying herself with Alyssa. They even encouraged a reluctant Wash to join in. Tamar grabbed his hand, and they danced to *All I Want For Christmas.* He lifted Tamar and spun her around and brought her down to him. She caught her breath just as he pressed his lips to hers. Alyssa giggled as she saw her father and Tamar kissing. Tamar broke the moment by grabbing Alyssa's and

Wash's hands and making them jump up and down to the music along with the crowds.

It was 7:30 P.M. when they left. Alyssa had danced so much she was soaking wet when Wash put her in her booster seat. Tamar was in such a time of reflection that she didn't realize she was home until he pulled in front of her house.

"Thanks, Wash, for the invitation. I had a wonderful time. Give Alyssa a kiss for me," Tamar said as she got out.

"You're most welcome. Thank you again for being so kind to her. It means a lot not just to her, but, to me also," he said as he placed a kiss on her forehead. The heat that radiated between the two caused her to pull away before she could not control his emotions.

"It was really no problem. She's such a beautiful and amazing child. She makes it so easy."

"Yes, she is," Wash agreed. "I wish we could spend the rest of the evening together, but I have plans. I guess I'll see you later."

"It's okay. I have something else going on later as well. I'm so glad we had a chance to hang out and get to know each other better. Guess I'll see you," Tamar said as she shut the door and headed inside.

Tamar was going out on New Year's Eve, thanks to Yolanda of course. Nonetheless, if this was Yolanda's way of getting her to meet someone, it was a no-go. She knew for herself that New Year's romances led to Valentine's heartbreaks. She'd already been there and done that—twice. Still, she pressed on. The voucher was good only one night, and it was at Owen Brennan's. The ambience and music alone, not to mention the delicious food, would be a good reason to get out. She looked in the mirror to make sure that her clothing choice was a good one. She smoothed royal blue sweater dress from the waist and glanced at the high heeled boots. It didn't scream desperate . . . too much.

As she opened the door to the restaurant, the sound of sultry jazz made her smile and uplifted her spirits. The thought of going out alone on New Year's Eve was daunting, and she was sure she would be the only single in the restaurant. She looked around and her thought was validated.

It took only a minute before she was approached by the waitress. She handed him her voucher, and he took her to her seat when she heard the all too familiar voice.

"Why, good evening ma'am. Nice to see you again. I'm sure it's purely coincidental."

Tamar shook her head, "Yep, looks like a *coincidence* to me. "Now I know what was in your envelope as well. Yolanda is just way too much. Where's Alyssa?"

"I left her with Marcus and Yolanda. Yolanda told me I would have a wonderful time tonight, and I should just let myself go because she had planned a special evening for me. Lo and behold." Wash walked around the table and placed a kiss on the top of Tamar's head.

"She's always pulling stunts like this, Washington. I'm so sorry. I'll go so you can enjoy yourself, and I'll just see if I can reschedule for a later date."

"No, no, no. That's fine. We're both here now. Let's seize the moment and enjoy it the best we can. Maybe we can use this time to actually get to know each other better. You look absolutely stunning, by the way."

Tamar blushed so hard she added extra light to the candle lit corner space that held their table. The waiter handed them the menus and requested their order. The two selected fried green tomatoes for an appetizer, the filet mignon for an entrée, and Banana's Foster for dessert. She made a mental note to thank Yolanda for putting them together. The waiter returned with their water and appetizers before the pair settled in well.

"Great service," Tamar said to the waiter. He nodded in gratitude and left the two.

"Tamar, you seem to have it all together. Why don't you have a man?"

Tamar almost spit out her water. "The reason I don't have man is because I'm not willing to settle for just anything. I don't lower my standards to raise anyone else's."

Her speech was interrupted by the ringing of her iPhone. Tamar answered the device, "Hi mom, are you guys back. Okay, see you then. Excuse me for the interruption. My parents are back from vacation."

"No. That's quite all right. As you were saying."

Tamar actually thought she could possibly change the subject. "Men want you to take care of them and their babies."

"Present company included."

"That's not what I meant, Washington. You have it together. Your situation is different. Your attitude and personality leave much to be desired."

Wash looked directly into Tamar's eyes and framed a teepee with his hands against his chin. "Am I really that bad, or am I just the first man you've come across that makes you feel intimidated?"

"I'm not intimidated, Mr. Washington. I just don't do chauvinism." All of sudden, Tamar's phone began to ring again. She answered once more. "Ma'am. I do not want to talk to you right. It doesn't matter where I am. Just know when I see you, you'll have plenty of explaining to do. You put this into motion because you're a control freak. I will punish you by not divulging any details about anything." Tamar ended the conversation with Yolanda and returned to Wash when his phone started ringing. "If it's Yolanda, don't answer." Washed shrugged his shoulders and let his phone go to voicemail.

"I know you think I'm a jerk. I'm not. I can't and won't apologize for my confidence. It's brought me this far. The cockiness, well, I can tone it down a bit."

"Gee, thanks," Tamar replied while trying to devour a strawberry cheesecake.

"Will you dance with me, Ms. Landry?'

Wash looked at her and shook his hand and gestured to the dance floor. The band started playing Luther Vandross' "If Only for One Night." Wash pulled Tamar close to him, and she nestled herself even closer. The scent of his Bvalgari cologne over took her, and she soon forgot herself.

"I could make you happy, change your perspective on men," Wash whispered into her ear.

Tamar breathed deeply. "You're still so raw Washington. You're hurting. I don't want to hurt you further, and I don't want to be hurt either."

"Call me Wash."

Tamar could've done a back flip on the dance floor. She was feeling lightheaded because of the scent of him. She wondered when his feelings towards her had changed. Her lips braised his chin, and he bent in to take in her essence. Then his phone rang, again.

He took Tamar's hand and turned her back to his chest. "Let's just tell her and get it over with."

"Okay. Just tell her we're together, but don't give any details. Make her suffer."

Wash giggled as he answered the phone. Tamar looked on as Wash's face began to contort.

"I'll be there shortly," he responded to the caller.

Tamar froze. "What's wrong? What's happened?"

"It's Alyssa. She had a high fever, and Yolanda was worried because she started sweating profusely and complaining she was aching all over. They took her to LeBonheur. I'm so sorry. I have to go."

"It's fine. Go to her. I'll call you tomorrow."

Wash placed a kiss on Tamar's forehead and allowed his lips to linger there momentarily. "I really enjoyed myself. Maybe we can do this again once Alyssa's better?" he asked.

"I'm counting on it. Give Alyssa a kiss for me," Tamar told Wash. He didn't hear her because he was running out of the restaurant.

Tamar sighed when she saw the waiter approach with the food.

"Could you please put the food in a carryout for me," He nodded as he walked away and returned with the carryout materials. Tamar's heart skipped a beat. She was falling for Wash and could no longer deny it. She was sad to see him leave, but she knew he had to see about his daughter. She just prayed that the little girl would be all right.

The next day, Marcus called and informed Tamar about Alyssa. The blood tests had revealed that Alyssa's white blood cells were elevated and upon further testing proved she had a common form of leukemia. Tamar knew all too well the pain parents went through when dealing with a sick child. Luckily, they had sent Alyssa to St. Jude, and Tamar was grateful. The sooner the hospital got to work on Alyssa, the better the outcome. Her heart ached for Wash. This news had to have cut like a knife. Tamar had to go back to work and not a moment too soon. Tamar met Yolanda and Marcus in the hallway. Marcus looked worried, and Yolanda was in tears.

"It happened so suddenly," Marcus informed Tamar. "She was fine when we put her down. Then she started whining and then came the full crying. We tried everything."

The tears became uncontrollably for Yolanda, and she broke down. Tamar went to her friend and held her. "It's okay, guys. It's not your fault. We see cases like this all the time."

"What's happening, Tamar?" Yolanda asked.

"She has acute lymphoblastic leukemia. It's better known as ALL. It's treatable and within two to three years, if God's will, she could be totally cured. It's the most common childhood cancer. How's Wash?"

Marcus grabbed the back of his head. "He's a mess. He called the grandparents. They're on their way."

"Good. He's going to need a good support system. That means you two have to pull yourselves together now," Tamar demanded, "I'm going to see her. I'll be back."

Tamar headed down the hallway and opened the door to Alyssa's room. She smiled when she saw the child looking directly at her. Alyssa was too weak to smile with her mouth, but Tamar saw it in her eyes.

"Hey, pretty girl," she greeted Alyssa.

Alyssa turned her head, her movement waking an apparently sleeping Wash sitting at the side of the bed. As he turned to face Tamar, her heart dropped. Marcus was right in his assessment. Wash was a mess. His eyes were red and puffy. She joined him at Alyssa's bedside and stroked his head. He buried his head at her waist and sobbed. Alyssa must have been given a good drug cocktail because she was going in and out, and she was now out.

Tamar raised Wash's head and tried to calm him, "Shh . . . Everything is going to be fine. She's at the right place at the right time. God is in control and he's going to carry you through this. That I can guarantee."

"I'm so scared. What if she doesn't make it, Tamar? I cannot lose her and remain on this side."

"Alyssa is strong. Her spirit is bright. She'll pull through this, and years from now, we'll all ponder the moment she was ever sick. I've seen her labs. I know the research. The success rate with treatment is high. She can be totally cured in a few years. Lean on your family and friends. We're here for you."

Wash's mouth moved, but no words escaped. He took Tamar's hand and did the only thing he could do: pray.

A month later…

Tamar had hung the last pink balloon. Grace and Jarvis were running around her house screaming to the top of their lungs. Her little helper, Aleena, had been with her from the beginning, giving her everything she asked for in hopes of receiving the strawberry cupcake that Tamar had promised her. Tamar grabbed the cupcake off the dining room table and watched as Aleena bounced in anticipation of its taste.

Mr. and Mrs. Landry were now standing before her with wide smiles. Tamar looked at them and returned the gesture. This was the day they had been eagerly awaiting for a while now. This would be the day they would meet Wash and Alyssa. Tamar had told them everything that had happened between her and Wash. Her mom had gushed like it was a story from a fairytale. Her father had asked when he could meet him. The time had come.

Alyssa's treatment was hard on her at first. Everybody held weekly prayer sessions for her. Pastor Hollins came by and laid hands on her. She had come full circle. She was being released from the hospital today and could now resume a somewhat normal life with limited activity. St. Jude had treated the leukemia vigorously and now with the aid of regular scheduled doctor visits and the right dosage of medication, Alyssa could be free from the cancer.

The doorbell rang, and, of course, Yolanda was all over it. Wash walked in carrying Alyssa, and Tamar could have fainted. He looked really good. Behind him was Wash's mother. She couldn't have looked more proud. Alyssa reached out for Tamar, and Tamar gently took the child from Wash's arms. Before she could give proper introductions, her mother beat her to the punch.

"You must be Washington," she acknowledged embracing him with a hug.

"Yes ma'am. I am. It's nice to meet you finally."

"You can call me Lorraine."

"Yes, Lorraine it's a pleasure."

Tamar's father walked up and gave Wash a firm handshake. "It's a pleasure to finally meet you Washington Parker," he said never breaking eye contact.

"The same to you, sir."

"Oh, please. No need for formalities. You can call me Mr. Drake Landry."

Wash looked mortified. Tamar held her head in shame while her mother, Lorraine, rolled her eyes. She couldn't believe her dad had used Wash's self-introductory strategy. Wash looked at the two women's actions, raised a brow, and turned to Tamar. He raised his hands in surrender. "I get it. I get it."

Tamar couldn't remember the last time she'd been so happy. Marcus entered the room with Grace and Jarvis in tow.

Grace screamed at the sight of Alyssa. "Nikki, you're finally home."

Tamar placed Alyssa down so she could hug her friend. The two girls squealed as they tickled each other.

"Mama," Grace said to Yolanda, "I'm so glad cancer let Nikki go. She's my friend, and I missed her so much."

Everybody in the room sighed. "I know, baby," Yolanda said trying to hold back the tears.

"It's okay, Mama," Grace said noticing the tears fall from her mother's face. "She's here, and we gonna get this party started. Hit it deejay!"

Marcus almost fell over Wash laughing as Drake hit the CD player button. From the speakers, Kelly Clarkson's "Stronger" blasted throughout the home. Aleena begin to shake her little bottom in excitement. Grace grabbed Alyssa's hand and began to sing with the music. "What doesn't kill you makes you stronger. Stand a little taller . . ." Soon everyone was up singing and dancing.

Wash pulled Tamar aside into the kitchen. He couldn't take his eyes off her, and she couldn't take hers off him.

"I want to thank you Tamar for making this so much easier. Who would've known those chance meetings would lead to this place in such a short period of time."

"I know, right? Just to think I couldn't stand you two months ago."

Wash chuckled and held her face between his hands. "I couldn't, I didn't think I'd ever feel this way about another woman again. You brought me back."

"Oh, Wash, you've shown me love in a different light. You've helped me to open up. I didn't realize I had become so withdrawn until I met you. Thank you." She squeezed him ever so tightly.

"Alyssa and I had a talk. She told me what she asked you on Christmas day."

Tamar stood still and waited for further details.

"She said you told her yes. I want to ask you the same question. Tamar Landry, can I keep you?"

"What?" Tamar whimpered.

"Valentine's Day is in a couple of weeks, and I want to know, will you be mine?"

Tamar didn't move. She just sobbed.

"Awww shucks, girl." Tamar and Wash looked up to see Yolanda standing in the doorway. "Must I do everything?" Yolanda asked. "Yes Wash, Tamar will be yours. Just not in that *True Blood* kind of way. And yes, you can keep her . . . that is until I need her. Then you'll have to turn her over until I've gotten what I needed accomplished. Deal?"

Tamar was astonished. Wash waited for her reaction to Yolanda's statement.

"Yolanda, for the love of God could you please stay out of this? I can speak for myself."

Yolanda peered at Tamar and waited. Wash laughed at the battle of the wills occurring between the two women.

"Wash," Tamar said looking into his eyes. "I will let you keep me as long as you keep me from Yolanda."

Wash spun her around and playfully pushed Yolanda out of the kitchen. The two held each other and basked in the glow of the wonders of a winter love.

Spring

Immortal Spring

By Vanessa Niki Davis

I couldn't sleep. I kept waking up, either from the baby's movement or from my dreams. Every time I closed my eyes, all I would see was Aaron's face. My dreams would not stop telling me that something was wrong with my husband. I've had these kinds of dreams before. Each night after we found out that he had been re-assigned to Afghanistan, until he kissed me near the loading dock of the U.S.S. Ronald Reagan. But after he kissed me and told me everything would be all right, the dreams stopped. I didn't know what was going on that night. It could've been the fried egg and toast I had for a midnight snack. Either way, it had me edging out what sleep I could get in the wee hours of the morning.

I was just feeling like I had fallen into a good restful sleep when my doorbell rang. *Ugh, who could be ringing my bell at…*I rolled myself over to look at the clock. *Seven-thirty in the morning!* I ignored the bell and then tried to close my eyes and go back to sleep. *Perhaps it was just a Jehovah's Witness getting their morning ministry in before it got too hot outside.* There was a second ring. "Go away," I whispered into my pillow. A few seconds later a knock. "Mrs. Trent, are you home?" I heard an unfamiliar voice say. Then, "Sophie, it's Jax. Open up." *What is Jax doing here?* I thought. "Just a minute," I yelled from my bedroom. "I'm just getting up." Tiptoeing into my slippers, I waddled out of bed and slipped my robe on as I exited the room.

I got to the door and looked through the peep hole. I was expecting only Jackson Scott, my best friend from childhood and Aaron's Navy Seal training partner. But it wasn't just him. As I opened the door, I saw there were four additional men. Two more all dressed up in suits and stars, and two in Navy fatigues.

Jax stepped aside. "Thank you, Lieutenant Commander Scott," said the older of the suited men. "Ma'am, may we come in?"

"It must be something important if you're ringing my doorbell at half past seven," I said. "Is Aaron all right?"

I expected a "yes, he's fine," but the younger naval officer just asked if they could enter. "Of course," I said, still sort of waking up. "Come in, gentlemen. I'm sorry for my rudeness. Would you like for me to put on some coffee for you all?"

"No ma'am. We won't be staying long." The two suited men walked in, but the men in fatigues stayed outside in perfect military stance.

"Ma'am, my name is Admiral Lennox," the older man said as he saluted, "and this is Captain Shipley." The younger of the two saluted and they both sat down in unison.

"What's this about? Is Aaron all right?" I asked once again.

"It's best if you sit down as well, Mrs. Trent," said Admiral Lennox

"What for?" I gave a stern look that demanded an answer. "Answer me. Is my husband all right?"

Jax was the last to enter. When I saw the folded flag in his hands, I knew my husband was dead. Then everything went black.

"Sophia?"

I thought it was Aaron, but the voice didn't sound like his.

"Sophia, come back to us hon."

"Jackson? Is that you? Where is Aaron?"

"He passed, Sophia. He's gone."

My eyes fluttered open, and I found myself lying on the couch. I saw Jax and Admiral Lennox crouched down at the front of my sofa staring at me. Captain Shipley was holding my wrist. I assumed he was taking my pulse.

"Are you going to be all right Mrs. Trent?" asked the Admiral. I couldn't tell him because I didn't know. I just stared at him, sort of in a daze. I wanted to yell and scream at these men who brought this news to my doorstep, but I couldn't talk. I slowly turned to look at Shipley, and he released my wrist. I tried to get up, but I tumbled back down to the couch. All I could do was hold my head in my hands and cry.

"Please leave my house," I said, almost inaudibly.

"If you would like to speak to someone, Mrs. Trent, you are welcome to come onto the base and talk to one of our counselors. That is your right as the widow," Shipley told me as he attempted to turn his callous tone into one of comfort.

"Please leave my house," I repeated, this time with more force.

"We have some personal effects of Lieutenant Commander Trent that we have to give to you."

I felt anger and sadness well up inside me. *Why can't these men just leave me alone to grieve? Why are they trying to make me take this in all in one day?* I looked at the three men standing in my house and could not bear to see their faces any longer.

"Get out of my house!" I screamed through my tears. "Just get out!"

I didn't have the strength to stand up and throw them out. Jax and the other officers left my house in a single file line, but not before they left Aaron's folded flag next to me on the couch and a small whisper from Jax. "I will come to check on you later Sophie. I'm sorry hon. I'm so sorry." I just hung my head and nodded as they left.

Regaining some of my strength, I slowly walked to the door and locked it. I looked at the clock. 8:30 A.M. It took all of an hour to change my life. I thought, at least at this time, these men, Lennox and Shipley, who are trained to show only bravery, honor, and stoic fortitude in a time of adversity would give a hint of sensitivity to the widow of one of their own fallen men. But it wasn't there. Yes, they tended to me after I passed out, but what would they have done if I hadn't? Would they have spent less time? Would they have even cared about how hurt I was? Questions filled my mind to the point of breaking. *What was I going to do?* I walked back to my bedroom and closed the door.

I stayed in bed all week. I didn't answer my house phone or cell. I barely got up to use the bathroom. Jax held to his word and had tried to call to check on me, but I didn't answer his calls. He even came by the house once or twice, but I didn't bother going to the door. I just lay under my down comforter and cried. *Hmph, comforter; who comes up with these names*, I pondered as I used one of its corners to wipe my welling tears. *Comforter. It's just an oversized, puffy blanket. To be honest, it didn't provide any comfort.* Yet as I lay there, I sank deeper and deeper underneath its warmth; hoping, wishing, praying that this ordeal was all just a horrible nightmare, but I knew it wasn't. So there I was, eyes closed, touching my unborn child, and trying my hardest to hold myself together as much as I could, but the thought of being a widow caused the tears to flow once more.

"Sophia?" I heard my mother calling from outside my bedroom door. "Sophia Marie Trent, if you don't open this door, I'm going to break it down. And you know I can do it, young lady!"

Jax must have called my parents to tell them the news, because I hadn't spoken to anyone since those men left my house. I just wanted to be alone. I couldn't deal with anyone, even my parents so soon. At that moment, I was regretting ever giving my mother a key to my house. "Please go away, Mom."

"Sophia, don't make a sixty-eight year old woman break down your bedroom door. Open up," she pleaded.

I sighed, swallowed hard, and got out of bed. I unlocked my door and then began to walk back to the safety of my bed. "The door is open, Mama. You can come in."

My mother walked in as I went to take a seat at the edge of my bed. I bowed my head as she took off her coat and hat and hung them on the hooks next to our closet. "Aw baby, I'm so sorry."

"So am I, Mama."

"Why didn't you call me and your father? If Jackson hadn't called, we would have never known," she said with concern.

"I don't know, Mama. I just needed time to organize my thoughts without people telling me what I should do." I looked up at her. Her arms were held out for a hug. I arose and fell into my mother's arms. That is when the reality of Aaron's death really hit me, and I sobbed loudly.

"Mama," I cried. "My husband is gone. My Aaron is gone."

"I know, baby. Let it out."

"They came last week to tell me he died overseas. I don't know how long they waited, but I had been having the bad dreams again, like the ones I was having for weeks leading up to him going there, and now, my worst nightmares have come true. It's not right, Mama. It's not right!"

"I know, Sophie, and you can grieve, but baby you gotta get yourself together for *your* baby that's on its way in just a few weeks. You certainly can't stay in this room, all cooped up, unwilling to face the world. You have to be strong despite this tragedy. And even though you say you wanted time to organize your thoughts, you still need people around, if only for support. Sophia, come stay with me and your father for a while. At least until you have the baby."

Sniffling, I gathered what composure I was able and gently pulled away from my mother. "No, mama, I need to stay here." I wiped my nose. "This was our home. This *is* our home, and I want our child to be born in it."

My mother gave me a strange look, then pulled me close, and hugged me again. "I don't really understand your reasoning behind this decision, but I know better than to question the thought processes of a pregnant woman," she said with a chuckle. "But as your mother," she cleared her throat, "I think you need someone in this house with you. How about this, how about I stay here with you until you tell me to leave."

"Mama, I really don't need . . ."

"Okay. Well, just to let you know, I wasn't asking you. I am telling you. I'm staying here at least until you have my grandbaby."

Sighing, I submitted to my mother's wishes and nodded in approval against her shoulder. I knew I had to be strong at this time too, but I sincerely didn't know how to do that. I needed my mother here.

"One more thing," my mother pulled away and looked at me with that serious Mama look, "we need to plan Aaron's homegoing service."

I shook my head. I just wanted this whole thing to end. "Mama, I haven't done anything for the past week since I found out. I know I need to plan something, but I'm not sure of what I want to do. I don't know if I want it at a church or if I want a small ceremony here. I know that I don't want a whole lot of people there, but as for anything else, I just don't know."

As I was talking, I heard the doorbell ring. I wasn't expecting anyone, but I knew I had been avoiding everyone, so I took my mother's hand and walked toward the family room to answer the door. I looked through the peep hole and was relieved to see Jax again. I really wanted to apologize for the way I acted toward him the previous week. I know he was only there to be a comfort to me. I just wasn't ready for anyone to do that yet. Thank God for faithful friends.

I opened the door and gave Jax a half smile.

"It's good to see you, Jackson."

"Hey, Sophia," Jax said as he walked in the door. "It's good to see you too."

"Jackson Scott, it's been too long. How are you?"

"Mrs. Olivia, looking lovely as ever," Jax said as he reached out to hug my mother. "I'm well. Hanging in there of course; but you know us military men."

"That I do, Jackson, and I wouldn't have it any other way." My mother smiled warmly as she took Jax by the arm and led him to the couch. "Can you stay for a while, or do you need to go back?"

"I can stay for a little bit, Mrs. Wallace. I just came by to check on our girl. You know she's been avoiding me. I really wanted to do this last week, just to make things easier, but," Jax looked at me, "I have some things of Aaron's that I need to give you."

I sighed and rolled my eyes. *Here we go again.* "What things do you have, Jax?"

"Some civilian clothes, letters, his wedding ring, things like that. Things that belong to you. I had them to give to you last week, but, well you know. They're in my car. I'll go get them. Be right back." Before I could say anything to protest, Jax was out of the door going to get Aaron's "things." I didn't want to take them. I wanted to tell him to just throw them all away. I put my hands on my tummy and looked at my mother. She held out her hand.

"Come into the kitchen, you two," she said with a half-smile. "I will make some breakfast."

I heard Jax come back into the house. "We are in the kitchen," I called out. He entered the kitchen carrying a large box with a small box on top of it.

"Where do you want them?" he asked.

"Just put the big box in that corner over there, and set the smaller box on that counter."

I was still unwilling to take the stuff, but since Jax went through all of the trouble to bring it to me, I shouldn't refuse. Plus, I might have wanted to keep the items within those boxes eventually.

"I'm making some breakfast. Would you like some?" my mother offered.

"No, ma'am."

"Well how about some tea? I am making tea as well."

"I'll pass, Mrs. Olivia. I'm more of a coffee drinker."

"OK." My mother went to the cabinet and got out the tea pot.

"What kind of tea would you like, honey?"

"Any kind is fine, Mama. I am more hungry than anything."
Jax took a seat next to me at the island as my mother steeped some black cherry tea.

"So Jackson, have you settled down since we last saw each other?" asked my mother, not looking up from her task.

Jax sighed hard and looked at me. I shrugged my shoulders. "No, Mrs. Olivia, I am still a single man."

"Haven't found the right woman to settle down with?"

"No, it's not that," he cleared his throat. "It's just that I don't think I am the marrying type. If anything, I am married to my job. The Navy really is my life."

"The Navy was Mr. Wallace's life too," my mother said as she placed two tea cups on the island. "That was until he met me. Maybe you just haven't met the right one."

"Maybe it's just not the right time, Mama, or maybe that's not what God has for him," I interjected, reaching for my tea cup. "You know what Paul said, 'God calls everyone to a specific vocation. Some are called to be married and some are called to be single. But no matter what, we are to do the best we can to glorify Him where He has placed us.' You never know, God could have called him to minister to his fellow seamen." I nudged Jax and smiled.

"As a matter of fact, Mrs. Wallace, I have been thinking about going to seminary," Jax said with a broad smile. "My commander said that I can go part time while on duty. Also, since I am eligible for discharge in about a year and a half, he said I can start going full time after that, and the Navy will pick up the bill. All I would have to do is agree to be available to be a chaplain two weeks every quarter. I have already led a number of people to Christ while here. Including Aar . . ." he stopped when he saw my mother shake her head.

"It's okay, Mama," I said smiling. "Jax introduced Aaron to Jesus, and then to me. He has been a true friend for a long, long time." I patted Jax on the hand.

"Well, what can I say to that?" my mom acquiesced as she sat at the island with us and passed me the tea pot. "If you feel a tugging from the Lord, who am I to say anything? Although, that *still* doesn't mean you can't get married one day," she said as she sipped her tea.

"You know, she won't give up until she finds you a wife." I shook my head. Jax sighed.

We sat there in silence for a few minutes. I don't know what my mom or Jax were thinking, but the mention of Aaron and how we met ran through my mind. I silently chuckled to myself and allowed a few tears to fall into my tea. My mother getting up to finish breakfast broke the quietness.

"So, Mrs. Olivia, will I see you at church this Sunday?" Jax asked. "You know it's Easter."

Easter Sunday. With everything going on, I totally forgot about the upcoming holiday. I usually sang in the Easter choir, but since I would be nearly due, and singing required me to be at practices as well as at the services standing for hours, the pastor thought that would be too much, so he told me to take this Easter off. I knew I should go, but I just didn't feel up to putting on a false smile while explaining to certain nosy people about Aaron's death, what I was going to do now, or anything like that. I passed on church last week and wasn't going to go this coming Sunday, but my thoughts shifted because of my mother's unexpected arrival and Jax's reminder that this Sunday was Easter.

"It's up to Sophia," my mother said as she handed me a plate of eggs, turkey bacon, and toast. "You already know what I think. Times like these are the ones we really need to be surrounded by praying people, but if Sophie doesn't feel up to it, then we might miss church this Easter."

"So Sophie," Jax looked at me with sincerity. "You know what your mom thinks, and you know my thinking is along those lines as well, but we are leaving the choice up to you."

I sighed. "We'll see how the week goes. I still talk to God. I can never stop doing that. It's mostly just the apprehension of dealing with some of the more nosy people at church. But we will see," I said looking up from my cup of tea.

"Well, I pray you have the peace of God the entire week so you are motivated to share in the joy of His resurrection day." Jax's watch began beeping. "Ugh," he said looking at the time, "it's time for me to relieve the night staff of their duty, but I will be back later to check on the both of you."

"Thanks, Jackson," I said as I stood up to see him out.

"Thank you for coming to visit, Jackson," my mother held her hand out to take Jax's arm.

"It was a pleasure, Mrs. Olivia."

We walked Jax to the door and said our goodbyes.

"I guess I should call your father to tell him that I am staying."

"You mean you didn't plan on coercing me into letting you stay?" I raised my eyebrow and smiled.

"Well, we discussed it, but you know how stubborn you are. Just like your father. We didn't know if you would say yes or no, so I told him that I would call him and let him know. He knows I was going to stay a few days, I just have to tell him now it's going to be about a month."

"You two," I shook my head. "Always plotting and planning, but I guess, this time, I am glad you did." My mother gave me a kiss on my forehead, hugged me tightly, and then called my father.

"Jason, pick up, it's me Olivia. Hey, honey. I am going to put you on speaker phone so that you can talk to Sophia too."

"Hey, baby," I heard my dad say.

"Hey, Daddy, how are you doing?"

"Just fine darling, I'm keeping active. But how are you? I am so sorry about Aaron. I wish I could be there too, but they needed another high ranking officer to oversee training here."

"I understand, Daddy. I am doing OK. I am glad that you sent Mama though. I thought I didn't need anyone here, but I really do."

"Oh, I didn't send her," my father laughed. "She was online making travel arrangements while talking with Jax. I just let her do her thing."

"Well, thank you anyway," I said, smiling at my dad's words.

"Jason," my mom joined the conversation. "I'm going to stay until after the baby is born. So I'm going to call the airline and tell them to delay the return ticket, or should I just cancel it and get my frequent flyer miles back?"

"I say cancel it, Libby. I mean it's not like you are losing any money. And you can use those miles for something else."

"Okay, well that's what I will do. We will let you get back to what you were doing honey. We'll probably call you later. I love you."

"I love you too, Olivia, and you too, Marie."

"I love you too, Daddy," I heard my father hang up the phone and then my mother and I went back into the kitchen.

"So, are you going to look through the boxes that Jackson brought over," my mother asked.

"I don't think I am ready yet, Mama," I said, sitting back down to my plate.

"Okay, baby."

Admiral Lennox and Captain Shipley came to my home to hand-deliver a plane ticket to Virginia for Aaron's so-called official funeral a week after their original visit, ironically, the day after Jax gave me all of Aaron's things that he said were mine. I had hoped I would not see those two men for a while, but there they were at my door again. Captain Shipley was rigid and seemed indifferent when he entered my house, but Admiral Lennox was surprisingly very cordial. He once again gave me his condolences and then handed me the first-class ticket and hotel information. When I asked about my mother, he told me that only immediate family were given accommodations, and since both of Aaron's parents were dead and he had no siblings, I was the only one. I explained to him that my family had become his family, especially my mother, who looked at the two men sadly, but with understanding of the procedure.

"Baby, it's all right," my mother said tugging on my arm. "We are going to have our own service, and I will be at that one."

"No, Mama. The Navy has taken too much from our family as it is," I protested. "You and Daddy were the closest thing to parents that Aaron had. We were *all* his family, and they are not going to deny us the right to say goodbye to him at his *official* funeral. Daddy may not be able to be here, but you are. The two of you were his family too! So they can at least make arrangements for you to attend also." I looked at Admiral Lennox. "Isn't there anything that can be done?"

"I will see what I can do, Mrs. Trent," he said.

He handed me the ticket, and then he and Captain Shipley left my house for the second time. Admiral Lennox returned later that day with another first class ticket and informed me that the ceremony would take place this Sunday at Arlington National Cemetery.

"This Sunday is Easter. Admiral Lennox…"

"Call me Wesley," he said with a comforting smile.

"Okay, Wesley, this Sunday is Easter. My mother and I were planning to attend church with Jax–I mean Lieutenant Commander Scott."

"I understand, Mrs. Trent, but scheduling special ceremonies at Arlington is difficult. If it isn't this Sunday, we would have to wait until next year, and the U.S. Navy felt that it would be too painful for the family members of the lost soldiers to relive a funeral."

"You have a point, Wesley," I sighed. "Maybe the United States Navy isn't as heartless as I thought." I half chuckled. "And you can call me Sophia."

He handed me the second ticket and then saluted.

"It is an honor to grant you this exception, Sophia. Your husband was a good and faithful soldier, but more than that, he was a good person. I had the honor of working with him on several occasions. He will definitely be missed."

I began to tear up. My mother came in from the kitchen and took my hand. Admiral Lennox—Wesley—left my house, and as I closed the door behind him I started to weep silently.

"So when do we leave?" my mother asked.

I looked at the ticket. "The flight is for Friday morning," I said.

"Okay."

My mother and I packed one large suitcase, with both of our clothes and necessities in it to save time and money on baggage fees, and left that Friday. The flight was pleasant enough but all I could think about was how much I didn't want it to be happening. I was en route to bury my husband. That thought still had me in a dream world. We hadn't even gotten a good ten years out, and now it's over. Not because we had fallen out of love with one another, but because Aaron had been killed serving his country. It was so unfair, and the more I tried to put the notions out of my mind, the more overwhelmed with grief I became. My baby moved inside me, sensing and feeling the emotions I was going through. When I felt the kick, I knew it was time to put a stop to the stress I was obviously feeling. My mom was right; I had to be strong for my baby. I made it up in my mind that from that point on, that's just what I was going to be.

We got off the plane and after we found our suitcase, my mother and I were greeted by a woman in a navy blue skirt suit and hat.

"Hello, my name is Lieutenant Amanda Bennett, and I will be your escort during your stay. If there is anything you need, Mrs. Trent, I am at your service."

"Hello, Lieutenant Bennett," I said with a smile, "and thank you. This is my mother Olivia Wallace."

"I am pleased to meet you, Lieutenant Bennett," my mother said as she shook the lieutenant's hand.

"Your ride is waiting for us outside." Lieutenant Bennett took our suitcase and carried it outside to a Lincoln Town Car.

"Wow, swanky," commented my mother. "Is this going to be our car the entire time we are here?"

"Yes ma'am," said Lieutenant Bennett as she put our suitcase into the trunk.

"Is there any way we can get something less showy?" I asked. "I mean, no offense to you or your commanding officers, but I'm not a flashy woman, and I can't imagine spending an entire weekend traveling in this."

"I'm sorry Mrs. Trent, but this is what Admiral Lennox ordered. If you want me to call him to ask for a different car, I will."

"No, no, this is fine," I said. I had given Wesley enough turmoil as it was. I figured that even though I was mourning the loss of my husband, my grief was no reason to make the things people were trying to do for me more difficult.

Lieutenant Bennett opened the door to let us into the car, closed the door, and then got into the passenger side of the car. Another officer was behind the driver's seat.

"Where to," he asked.

"Take us to the hotel, Ensign Loo. I am sure these two ladies would like to rest for a bit. Is that all right with you Mrs. Trent?"

"Can we stop to get something to eat?" I asked. "I couldn't eat the food the flight attendant served on the plane, so the baby has been temperamental since this morning."

"The baby has been temperamental, Sophie? Why are you blaming that baby for your irritability?" My mother taunted and then gave me a look.

"Well, our personalities are intertwined for the time being. I am hungry so I know he or she is hungry." I nudged my mom and giggled a little.

"When are you due?" Lieutenant Bennett asked.

"My official due date is April twenty third," I said beaming. "However, because this is our first baby . . ." I hesitated and bit my lip, trying to hold in the flood of emotions that overtook me as I made that statement. "I mean, since this is my first pregnancy...the doctor said that we . . . I . . . might . . .," I couldn't get myself to continue without choking up.

"It's okay, Mrs. Trent," Lieutenant Bennett said. "If it's too difficult for you to talk right now, then we can just go get you something to eat. What are you in the mood for?"

"I think I just want to go to the hotel," I said sniffling. "We can get something to eat a little bit later, when my mom and I are settled in."

"Understood. Loo, will you take us to the Embassy?"

We drove to the hotel in silence. I immersed in my thoughts of Aaron while my mother snoozed a bit, tired from our flight. The Lieutenant did not say anything else to me. I figured she thought she had said enough. I wanted to talk to her about our baby; I was so happy to be pregnant. It was just that some things got to me when I thought about our baby, but I was so proud to carry the greatest gift Aaron could have given me before he died.

We arrived at the Embassy Suites thirty minutes after we arrived in Virginia. Ensign Loo got our suitcase and helped us out of the car, while Lieutenant Bennett made sure that we were checked in properly. When we walked in, a bellhop took the luggage from Loo and then took my arm.

"Mrs. Trent, Mrs. Wallace, if you will come with me, I can take you to your room."

"Thank you," I said, "but where is Lieutenant Bennett, the officer that walked in before we did?"

"She is making further arrangements and will join you shortly. She advised me to get you settled in."

"OK, then lead the way."

By this time, I was regretting my rash decision to wait to eat. I was starving. As we approached the elevator, I asked the bellhop if he knew of any places to get a quick bite to eat.

"Well, Mrs. Trent, it all depends on what you want."

"Something close, cheap, and good," I said as we got onto the elevator.

"Something healthy," my mother said. I scrunched my face.

"Well, from my understanding, all of your expenses will be paid for. So you can order room service, go to the Crystal Grill on the first floor, or there is a Subway a few blocks from here. They do deliver to this hotel if you do not wish to drive. There is a Whole Foods nearby, and they have ready-made food for you to choose from. Also, there is a list of local restaurants in your room."

We got out of the elevator on the second floor. The bellhop used our key card to open the door. My eyes widened upon entering suite 216. It was enormous and so nicely decorated.

"This is so beautiful," my mother said.

"It was newly remodeled about two years ago," the bellhop said proudly.

"Well," my mom smiled and said, "they certainly did a wonderful job."

The bellhop set our suitcase down near the first bed. "I will let you ladies get settled in."

"Thank you, I'm sorry, but we didn't get your name," I said as I handed him a ten dollar bill from my purse.

"Julian," said the bellhop.

"Thank you Julian. You have been so very helpful. We will certainly take everything you have told us into account. Actually, we better do it soon before this baby gives me what for."

"Thank you, Mrs. Trent. The Lieutenant should be up soon." After all of the customary sentiments, Julian the bellhop, left.

"He was awfully nice," my mother said as she opened the suitcase.

"Yes he was. Now let's get something to eat."

My mother looked up from what she was doing and glared at me. When she saw my "hungry child" look, she laughed, closed the suitcase, and walked toward me. As we were walking out of the door to go downstairs, we were greeted by Lieutenant Bennett.

"Hello ladies. I came to tell you that we are running a tab on all of your food expenses. Order what you want from room service or the restaurant downstairs. If you spend any money on food, please be kind enough to bring us the receipt, so that we can reimburse you. The hotel is paid for as well. If you need anything, I will be in suite 229 down the hall."

"Thank you Lieutenant," I said. "We are actually on our way to go get something to eat. Would you like to join us?"

"Not this evening. I'm sorry Mrs. Trent. However, you and your mother have a nice early dinner. If you need a ride, please contact Ensign Loo, and he will take you wherever you would like to go."

Lieutenant Bennett handed me a card with her cell phone number as well as a number to reach Ensign Loo written on it. I took the card and put it in my purse. My mother and I said our goodbyes and went toward the elevator.

We decided to take Julian's suggestion and try out the Crystal Grill. The hostess seated us quickly; however, when we got the menu, my mom became a little uneasy.

"The food is kind of pricey," my mom said, covering her words with the restaurant's menu.

"Oh, Mama, the prices aren't that bad. Plus, the lieutenant told us to order what we want," I said squirming, trying to find a comfortable position in my seat.

"I don't know, Sophie. Maybe we should just get something we know, like Subway."

"Is it the price of the food or the food itself that you are unsure about?" I asked. "You are always telling me that we should visit different places and try new things. I mean, this isn't really different or new food, but it *is* in a different place. It's just a little more expensive than what we may be used to."

"I guess so. Well, what do you want to do, Sophia?"

"I wanna eat. So whether we are going to eat here or somewhere else, I'd like to get it settled."

"Well, let's stay here then."

I was relieved that my mom chose not to explore around to find somewhere to eat. I was starved and could hardly wait another second to begin eating. The waitress' timing was incredible.

After we ate, we went back to the suite. As soon as we got in the door, tiredness hit me, and I was immediately sleepy.

"I'm going to go to sleep for a while, Mama" I said as I crawled into the bed that was farthest from the door.

My mother laughed. "All that rich food got you knocked out, huh?"

"I think it's just because I've been up super early the past few days. It's catching up with me. It could be the time difference too."

"No it's the food," my mom giggled.

"Oh hush, Mama," I said as I kicked off my shoes and slipped my feet under the covers.

I didn't plan to, but I slept until the next morning. I woke up to the sun shining in my face and still wearing the clothes I had on the previous day. I looked over at the clock which read nine thirteen in the morning. *Ugh, that means it's 6:13 in California.* I got out of the bed, closed the drapes and then slipped under the covers to try to go back to sleep. In what seemed like thirty seconds later, the phone rang. Loudly. I looked over at the clock. 9:35 AM. I reached over and answered the phone.

"Hello, Mrs. Trent? This is Lieutenant Bennett. I wanted to call and let you know that we will be coming to get you in about an hour."

"Okay, where are we going?"

"I have orders to take you to meet Admiral Lennox."

Wesley is here. I wondered why he wanted to meet with me, but I didn't think further on it. "Okay, thank you, Lieutenant. I will see you in an hour."

I hung up the phone and then rolled out of bed. I walked over to my mother's bed to wake her up.

"Mama, get up. Lieutenant Bennett will be here in an hour to take us to see Admiral Lennox."

My mother slowly opened her eyes and looked at me. Then yawned, stretched and blinked her eyes a few more times. She scratched her head and then spoke.

"What?"

I couldn't do anything but laugh. "Lieutenant Bennett will be here in an hour to take us to meet with Admiral Lennox. You have to get up."

Upon hearing the news that the Lieutenant was on her way, my mother's eyes opened wide. She shook her head, got out of bed, and headed for the bathroom. A minute later, she came out, reached inside of a drawer, pulled out a shower cap, and then went back in.

While my mother showered, I had a thought. I called the Lieutenant's room.

"Hello, Mrs. Trent."

"Hi, Lieutenant Bennett, I had a question. What do I wear? I mean is this a formal meeting or casual?"

"It's brunch. Admiral Lennox just wanted to meet with you to go over a few details before the funeral tomorrow. Nothing too big. He just wanted to get you up to speed on how tomorrow's events will go."

"Oh, okay, thank you. I'll see you in an hour."

I hung up the phone and then continued to get my clothes out of the closet. I love my mother. I saw that she had taken everything out of the suitcase and organized them in the closets and drawers while I slept last night. I took out everything I would need for after I got out of the shower and then patiently waited for her to come out of the bathroom.

At exactly 10:35 there was a knock at the door. "Mrs. Trent, Mrs. Wallace, are you two ready to go?"

"Yes, we are coming out now," I said as I opened the door.

Lieutenant Bennett and Ensign Loo smiled as we walked out.

"How did you sleep, ladies," asked the Lieutenant.

"Very well," I said. "How about you two?"

"I slept well. How did you sleep, Loo?"

"Like a baby, ma'am."

The short exchange between the two made me laugh inside.

"That's good to hear," I said. "Shall we go?"

We met Admiral Lennox at a restaurant called Whitlow's on Wilson. The restaurant had a wonderful Saturday brunch menu that had a variety of different food combinations. It was a buffet, so we could have our choice of everything they had to offer. While eating my spinach omelet and fruit, Wesley began speaking.

"Sophia, Mrs. Wallace, the reason why we brought you here is because we didn't want anything to be a surprise."

"I understand, Wesley," I said.

He explained to us that Aaron had chosen to be cremated and because of this reason, they would not have a pall bearing ceremony. There is a separate ceremony for the servicemen who chose to be cremated; however, it is all done in the same day over the course of a few hours. There will be a gun salute and a flag ceremony where all of the relatives of the fallen will be given an American flag. Afterwards, there is a reception that we will have to attend where the President would say something about the soldiers who gave their lives for the United States and officially award their families if they received any medals. He also told us that Aaron was receiving a few awards.

"Which awards is he receiving?" My mother asked.

"He is receiving the Purple Heart, The Navy Cross, and the Congressional Medal of Honor."

"You are giving my son-in-law the Medal of Honor?"

My mother gasped and nearly passed out at the news that Aaron would be receiving the Medal of Honor. I looked at her because I really didn't understand why it was such a big deal. We have a curio full of Aaron's medals, trophies, and other military honors. I really didn't know it was that big of a thing. After brunch, I decided I would look up some information on all of the medals that my Aaron would be receiving. After reading the information about the medals, I was in awe. I understood why my mother reacted the way she did. My Aaron was going to receive the highest honor that could be bestowed upon any soldier in the United States Armed Forces. I started to cry.

The next day, my mother and I woke up before sunrise. We prayed together. We thanked God for not only sending Jesus to die for our sins, but also for raising Him on this day so we also have a chance at eternal life. After we prayed and read the resurrection story from the book of Luke, we got ready for the funeral to be held later that morning. Around seven thirty, Lieutenant Bennett came to the door to escort us to the funeral. We got into the car without speaking and drove in silence to Arlington National Cemetery.

It was a beautiful ceremony. Just as Wesley had said, they brought all of the soldiers who were to be buried around to the place where they were to be laid to rest, presented all of the soldiers who were cremated to their appropriate family member, gave a twenty-one gun salute in honor of all of the fallen soldiers, and presented a folded American flag to a representative of the families. Then we went to the White House, where President Obama gave a stirring speech honoring all of the fallen and officially presented the awards that were to be given that day. After the services, we headed back to the hotel to pack our things for the plane ride back to California. Jax was waiting at the airport to meet us when we got home. He drove us back to my house and then went back to the base for work, but not before he said he would return.

My mother walked straight into the kitchen as soon as I opened the door and started brewing some tea. I sighed because I knew what that meant. Whenever my mom starts brewing tea out of the blue, she is thinking deeply about something and wants to talk about it. I was in somewhat high spirits until that moment because I knew that she may want to talk about what we were going to do here for Aaron's homegoing. I wanted to put something together for my husband, but after just coming home from one funeral, I didn't have the energy to talk about organizing another. I went to my room, changed my clothes, and got into bed.

I woke up a few hours later and walked out of my room toward the kitchen. I found my mother sleeping on the couch still dressed in the clothes that she wore that afternoon and her cup of tea sitting on a coaster on the end table. I didn't want to wake her, but it was almost 8 o'clock, and we hadn't eaten anything since the reception at the White House. I needed something to eat and, I figured that she did too. I went into the kitchen and grabbed the binder Aaron and I kept which had most of the local restaurant menus inside. I flipped through it, looking for something that I would like and that my mom could enjoy when she awakened.

I decided to order something from the Mediterranean Café, a really good restaurant in the area. As I was dialing the telephone number, I got a text message from Jax letting me know he would be coming over in about fifteen minutes. I sent a reply asking him if he would like anything from the restaurant. He said he would pass on the bunny food, but that he would just pick up a burger on the way over. I was glad that he had sent a text message because if he were here, he would have seen me roll my eyes. I completed my order and then went to the kitchen to warm up the tea that my mother had made earlier.

While I was heating up the tea at the stove, I heard my mother move around and wake up. She walked into the kitchen rubbing her eyes.

"Ah! Sleeping Beauty has awakened."

My mother laughed a little and sat at the island. I brought her a tea cup and poured her some of the re-heated tea. I poured myself a cup and took a seat at the island across from her.

"Jax is on his way over. Also, I ordered some food so that should be here shortly too."

"You ordered something healthy I hope."

"I ordered something from a local Mediterranean restaurant."

My mother smiled at the idea that I actually took it upon myself to order something healthy. I just shook my head and smiled. While my mom sat doctoring up her tea to her liking, she looked over at me.

"Are you ready to talk now?"

"I guess so," I said sighing.

"If you aren't, let me know."

"No, if I don't organize something, it's not going to get done. It's just hard for me, you know. I just thought that I would be able to grow old with him, not sitting here by myself planning his funeral."

"You are not by yourself, Sophie. We are all here for you."

I shook my head. "But my husband is not here. I'm still trying to wrap my mind around Aaron being gone."

I took a deep breath, trying to hold back the tears. All I could do was shake my head to fend off the sadness. I heard the doorbell ring, but I couldn't get myself up to go to answer it. My mother got up from her cup of tea and went to the door. When the door opened, I smelled the distinct scent of a double-double from In-N-Out Burger, and a minute later Jax came walking into the kitchen. He also had our food from the Mediterranean Café. He set it on the island in front of me.

"Your bunny food, Madame."

"Thanks, Jax, but how did you get it?"

"Ran into the delivery guy at the door. He said he was in a hurry. Since I said I was coming in, he handed it to me."

"Really? You could've been anyone and he just handed over food I had already paid for? I'm calling over there now to tell them about themselves."

"That's only the hunger talking," my mom said as she walked back into the kitchen and took her seat.

I frowned and reached for the bag. In all actuality, it was the hunger talking. I was in no mood to yell at anyone, let alone over some food. He was probably a young guy who was running late on his deliveries. I took a deep breath and opened the bag.

Against my hurt feelings, we talked about Aaron's funeral. I decided I didn't want to hold it at the church, simply because I wanted it to be quick and small. We would hold it here at the house a week from the upcoming Saturday. Jax agreed to call the pastor to make arrangements. We made a list of the people whom we wanted to be there; my mother and I would call everyone in the morning. After we organized everything, Jax took his to-do list and went home.

"I know it won't make you feel as good as if you didn't have to do this, but I tell you Sophie, you will feel better after you get this part behind you. You'll see," my mother said rubbing my hand.

"I hope so."

After the discussion and the food, I was exhausted all over again. I put up the leftover food, washed the dishes, and then went to my bedroom to go to sleep.

When I awoke in the morning, I began making the arrangements for Aaron's funeral. My mother made a few of the calls while I organized the program. I had decided to bury Aaron's wedding ring underneath our oak tree in the back yard during the ceremony. I knew it was in the smaller box that Jax brought over the previous week. I took a deep breath and went to the kitchen counter to get it.

I sat at the island and opened the box. Inside I found his wedding ring and other jewelry, the sonogram picture of our baby that I sent to him months ago, and some envelopes wrapped in a dark green velvet ribbon. I moved the ribbon to the side and saw that there were about five letters, all addressed to me. Tears started to stream down my cheeks. I took the ring and the picture out of the box, put the ribbon back on the letters, and closed it, too broken up to think about what Aaron had written to me.

We had Aaron's homegoing in our rose garden. It was a small ceremony with just our close family and friends. I couldn't bear to have a huge event like the one the US armed forces held at Arlington Cemetery. The pastor of our church gave a wonderful sermon from the third chapter of Ecclesiastes and correlated it to my favorite passages in the eighth chapter of Romans. When we gave time for people to speak about Aaron, they only said wonderful things. I knew how much he had touched my life, but I had no idea how much he had touched the people around him until everyone started telling their stories about how they met Aaron or how he made a difference in their lives.

I buried a box containing our baby's first sonogram, one of the flags the Navy gave me, a few of his medals, and his wedding ring. I sprinkled his ashes around our oak tree and after a prayer, the funeral was over. I didn't have a reception, but some of the old school invitees brought food for my mother and me. My mother was right as always; after the funeral was over and everyone had left, I did feel a little better now that part of grieving was behind me.

Jax stayed behind after the funeral to help my mother and I clean up. "Thanks so much Jackson," my mother said. "We would have been up for hours cleaning."

"It's no problem, Mrs. Wallace. Anyway, I told the pastor that I would haul these chairs back to the church later on today."

"Don't listen to him Mama," I joked. "You know you just stayed behind to eat some of this food the church mothers left here."

My mom scolded me through the laughter she tried to hide. "Now, Sophia Marie, you be nice."

"It's ok, Mrs. Olivia." He looked at me. "I'll have words with your daughter later."

I looked at him sideways, and he winked at me. I smiled. It was nice not feeling sad after such an occasion. While Jax went to collect the chairs and take down the decorations we had in the back yard, my mom and I stayed in the kitchen and put away the food.

"I have to admit Mama, you were right," I said as I put my head on her shoulder.

She placed her hand on my head and asked, "Feeling better, Sophie?"

"Not back to where I want to be, but surprisingly not where I thought I would be after everything that has happened." I walked over to the refrigerator.

"If you are in a better place, then that is good."

"I'm in an OK place," I smiled at her.

Jax came back into the house with a box filled with the decorations from outside. "Where do you want me to put these?"

"Will you set them in the study please? I want to look through a few of the items in the box," I said.

"Well after this, I have to be on my way. I need to have the chairs back to the church before 6 o'clock."

"Thanks again, Jackson," my mom said. "I made a plate in here for you, so make sure you pick it up before you leave." Jax smirked at me as he walked into the study.

"OK, that's it," Jax said as he entered the kitchen rubbing his hands together. "Where's that plate?"

"See, Mama, I told you." I squinted my eyes at Jax who stuck his tongue out at me.

"Y'all haven't changed since you were children," my mom said shaking her head. She walked over to Jax, who was lifting the top off of his plate to see what was on it.

"I'll see you soon, Jackson. I have to go lie down now." She kissed Jax on the forehead and went to the bedroom.

"Are you sure you're OK?" Jax asked as I led him to the door.

"I'll be ok," I said half smiling.

He put his plate down on the table and gave me a big hug before I opened the door. Then he took my hand. "I want you to know, that if you ever need me for anything, I'll be here for you." He picked up his plate, gave me a warm smile, and left.

I had a dream about Aaron that night. He was in our rose garden holding the box that I had buried. I went and sat next to him as he opened it, but it didn't seem like he could see me. He admired the medals and smiled. Then he picked up the sonogram picture of our baby and began to cry. I wanted to comfort him, but felt that I couldn't right then. When I woke up, I decided to open the large box that Jax had brought over.

The next morning after breakfast, my mother and I moved the box into the family room and I sat on the floor to sift through its contents.

"Will you be all right, Sophie?" my mother asked.

"I think so. If it gets to be too painful, I will stop."

My mother sighed "Okay honey, then I'm going to go to the store to pick up some groceries. I'll be back soon."

"Okay, Mama. I love you."

"I love you too, baby." My mom gathered her purse and the car keys and left.

The smell of Aaron's Nautica cologne filled my nostrils as I opened the box. I did my best to hold back my tears as I went through all of his clothes and shoes, still looking brand new in the boxes. I always liked Aaron's style and taste in clothing. He was never really flashy; he just liked what he liked and looked nice in whatever he wore. He never wanted me to buy clothes for him, but he always commented on and bought clothes that he thought I would look good in. He spoiled me that way.

Because he did that for me, I always found ways to keep him smiling. I never thought I would do the things I did for Aaron for any man, but because he was so good to me, I decided I was going to be good to him. I had never cooked anything for anyone other than myself; but shortly after we became an item, I took a cooking class because I knew he liked good food.

Aaron wasn't fond of a whole lot of make-up and that was fine with me because I didn't really wear any. He said he appreciated my natural beauty. What he didn't tolerate was my toes not being done. He always said my feet were too beautiful not to have my feet done, so I always made sure that I got a pedicure either every week or every two weeks as my money would allow. I also wore toe rings and ankle bracelets to make my feet look more attractive.

We had our share of good and bad times. We fought, we made up, and we had our times of indifference, but through everything, he was there for me, and I was there for him. I didn't believe in soul mates before Aaron, but after we met, I could truly say I was wrong, because he was definitely a mate for my soul. All the thoughts of Aaron and the times we shared got to me. I had to stop. I put everything back into the box and left it on the floor.

I went to the kitchen and made some tea. As I waited for the water to boil, I sat at the island and my eyes caught the smaller box Jax had brought sitting there. It still had some of Aaron's necklaces and his watch in it. It also had the letters inside. I didn't want to, but something was compelling me to read the letters. I reached into the box and took the package of letters wrapped in the green ribbon out. I opened the first one.

Dearest Sophia,

If you are reading this letter, it means that I have died. I know it's hard to believe and difficult to deal with, but know that I lived with a purpose and I died for a purpose. Although it may not seem like it now, it was God's perfect design and for that, know that I am grateful...

I stopped reading. *How dare he write me a letter like that?* I thought. *What about our plans? I wanted to spend the rest of my life with you. I wanted to grow old with you. I wanted us to see our children...children, plural, more than one... grow up and have their own families. And now what? I have to raise our one child by myself. What kind of plan is that?* I was so hurt and angry at Aaron's words, I was beside myself. I couldn't stop crying. I didn't want to read another word. I took all of the letters and ripped them into pieces. I put them in the trash can and then took the trash out to the garbage bin on the side of our house.

I had another dream about Aaron. This time, I saw him playing with a little girl in our front yard. They were having a tea party and I was in the kitchen looking at them through the window. He looked so happy. I thought about going out there and taking a picture to capture the moment, so I went to the bedroom to get the camera, but when I returned they were gone. Then I woke up.

I couldn't get back to sleep, so I decided to get up and sit in our back yard to ponder what my new dreams meant. It was just after midnight when I walked into the garden. I don't know what I was expecting to find; they were only dreams, but they both seemed so real. I breathed in the surprisingly warm spring air and smelled the nearby ocean, which made me miss my husband even more. I looked at the tree where I sprinkled Aaron's ashes and buried his wedding ring. I was startled to find the letters he had written.

I know I had taken those letters and not only ripped them up, but threw them into the garbage. Yet there they were, in the envelopes, neatly tied up in the evergreen ribbon, and lying underneath the tree as if nothing had happened to them. I approached the letters. The envelopes were crumpled, but intact. I opened one of the letters. It was all in one piece, but I could see the marks from where I had ripped it. All of the letters were like that. I thought I was in the twilight zone. Either that or someone was playing a very morbid, very hurtful trick on me.

"What is going on," I whispered. "Why did You bring me out here, Lord?" I looked into the sky.

I didn't know if I was expecting God to send me an answer right then and there or what. All I knew was that it was too soon to pull at my heart, the way all of these events had been. I was overly pregnant and so out of any kind of understanding that the Lord had endowed me with. I sat down on our garden bench and started praying:

"Lord, I don't know what is going on or what You are allowing to occur in my life, but I just pray that I stay in Your divine will. Please forgive me of my sins and continue to give me peace. Please also give me wisdom to be able to raise my and Aaron's child the right way. In Jesus' name I pray, amen."

After my prayer I felt better. I grabbed a hold of the end of the bench and got up to go back into the house, but not before I did something with those letters. I held onto the tree and knelt down to pick up the package of letters. I walked in and prepared to put them into the shredder. I took the letters into the study and placed them on the desk. Suddenly, I was overcome with sleepiness. *I will shred them later on today, after I get some sleep.* I went back to my room, yawning and preparing to sleep for hours.

When I went back to sleep, I had another dream. I was back in the rose garden and I saw Aaron facing the oak tree. I walked toward him, and he turned around, like he heard me walking. I stopped, and he looked at me.

"Mariposa," he said.

I started crying. I had not heard him call me that in almost a year, and now it would never happen again. I felt fear because I knew I was dreaming. I thought that if I said anything to him, then he would go away, and the dream would be over; and I wanted this dream to last as long as it could. He walked over to me and took my hand. I held my breath.

"Why did you stop?" he asked.

I didn't talk. I just stared at him, his honey brown eyes staring back at me. He was always able to leave me speechless with his stare, but now staring into his eyes, I felt an empty sadness, and more tears fell. He touched my face and wiped my tears.

"Please talk to me Sophie."

"What do you want me to say, Aaron?" I said. I could've kicked myself after I said that. *There had to be other things I could have said to him, and that stupid, sarcastic question was all I could think of?*

Aaron just laughed.

"I mean, I miss you, Aaron."

"I am here now, Sophia."

"But you're not. You're a dream. A figment of my now twisted imagination. I don't know why I keep doing this to myself."

Aaron pulled me close and kissed me softly. "Everything is going to be all right, Mari, you'll see."

I woke up and cried.

Later on that morning, I talked to my mother. I had to tell her about the letters, the strange dreams I had, and the way that all of these events were making me feel.

"He wrote me letters, Mama" I said as I sipped on my tea. "About five of them. I read the first lines of the first letter, and I couldn't read anymore. He wrote it like he knew he was going to die."

I took one of the letters from its envelope and showed it to her.

Looking at the crumbled letter, she asked "Why does it look like this?"

"I ripped all the letters up and threw them in the trash. That's the crazy part. Later on last night, after another dream, I went out into the garden, and they were under the tree, like nothing had ever happened to them. I mean they looked like something had happened to them, but they were repaired somehow."

"Did you pray about it, Sophie?"

"I did the first time, but after I had the last dream, all I could do was cry."

"Well baby, I think that you should continue to pray. The Lord doesn't allow these things to happen for nothing. Ask Him what He would like for you to get out of these experiences." As I was about to reply, the doorbell rang. I walked out of the kitchen to see who it was and was surprised to see Jax this late in the morning. He must have had the day off.

"Listen Sophia, I'm sorry for just dropping by like this," he said as he walked in the door, "but I woke up thinking about you and I have been all morning. I had to come see if you were okay."

"You sound like you're out of breath," I said chuckling. "Did you run over here?"

"Ha ha," he said. "As a matter of fact, I did. I was on my morning jog and decided to take a detour to your house."

"Well you should know, after all these years, that you dropping by unannounced is never a problem. I'm actually doing better than I thought I would." I raised an eyebrow. "What's up with you? You have never apologized for stopping by. Something on your mind?"

My mother overhearing our exchange came out of the kitchen. "Hey, Jackson. Sophia, I'm going to take a walk for a bit. I'll see you later."

Jax walked over to the couch and sat down. I followed. "You look distressed, Jax. You want me to make you some coffee or something?"

Jax took a deep breath. "No Sophia, I'm all right I think."

"You think?" I gave him a confused look.

"Yeah, just come sit. I need to talk to you."

The seriousness in his voice concerned me. "What is it, Jax? Are you ok?" I asked as I sat down next to him.

"I've just been thinking a lot lately," he said as his voice became lighter.

I smiled. "There has been a lot of that going on around here too."

As I was about to tell him about the dreams I had, he looked at me with that serious look again.

"I love you, Sophia."

My smile grew a little wider, "I love you too, Jax. You're the best friend I have." I took Jax by the hand.

"No, I mean I am *in* love with you."

The smile on my face was slowly replaced with a look of bewilderment as I let go of his hand. "What?"

"I am in love with you Sophia. I have been for years. Even before I introduced you to Aaron."

"Why are you telling me this? Why now? Of all the times for a confession, why now?"

"Believe me, I know it's bad timing," he said trying to reach for my hand again.

"Oh, you think," I said angrily, not letting him touch me.

"Sophia, let me explain," he pleaded.

I sat there with a sour look on my face. "I'm listening, Jackson."

"I thought I had gotten over my feelings for you a long time ago, but when I came over to bring Aaron's stuff, your mom said something that made me think."

"So are you telling me it's my mom's fault?"

"No, that's not what I'm saying. I'm saying that it's my fault I never told you. And then when you and Aaron got married, I decided I was just going to be your friend. But when your mom was asking me why I wasn't married and we were talking about me becoming a minister and how supportive you were of me, it got me thinking about how supportive you have always been of me and that's what I loved about you and our friendship. It also had me thinking that the reason I have never gotten married is because every girlfriend I have had since we first met, I've always compared them to you. I've been looking for that support that you have always given me."

"And this was such an opportune time, huh?" I said still skeptical. "Your best friend's husband dies, and you move in with this?"

"It's not like that, Sophie," Jax said sadly

"Then what is it like?"

"I'm hurt too, Sophia. Don't think that I am not. He was my friend too. And I don't want you to think that I was just waiting for my opportunity, because I wasn't. I don't know what would have happened if Aaron hadn't died. These feelings probably would have never been stirred up again. However, the fact is that they have been, and I needed to tell you if I am going to continue to be the friend that you need me to be. I couldn't let the feelings that I have for you cloud my judgment or cause me to say or do the wrong thing down the line."

I looked down, sort of embarrassed. "So what happens now? What do you want me to say?"

"I don't know what happens now, Sophie. I'm not expecting anything. I just needed to tell you."

I sighed deeply. "Well, I appreciate you for being honest with me."

"You're my best friend. I can't be anything else to you."

My smile returned as I got up to go into the kitchen. "Do you want something to eat?"

"No, that's OK, Sophie. I better go now, but I'll be by later."

"OK." I walked him to the door, and then he was gone.

Later on that evening, Jax called. He told me that he was a little nervous about coming by the house after what we talked about that morning.

"I understand, Jax, but you know we are still friends."

"I know, Sophia, it's just…"

He didn't have to say anything else. I completely understood where he was coming from. After a few seconds of silence, he cleared his throat.

"I wanted to know if I could still go with you and your mom when the baby is born."

"Of course, Jackson," I said. "Why would I change my mind about that?"

"I don't know."

"Who else am I going to punch and scream at while I'm pushing out this baby? Surely not my mama. She would whoop me while I'm on the table," I giggled.

Jackson's nervousness subsided and he let out a small chuckle and sighed. "You really do know how to make me feel better."

"Okay, that sounded weird, but I won't hold that against you. You just be ready to go, because the baby can come any time."

"You can count on me, Sophie."

"I better be able to," I said. "I'll talk to you later. Right now, I need to try and get some sleep."

I had another dream. This time, I saw Aaron and Jax on the beach, standing by and looking out into the ocean. As I ran to meet them, Aaron was instantly right in front of me.

"You know he loves you," were the first words out of his mouth. I stood there dumbfounded.

I lowered my head and nodded. "I know. He told me this morning," I said.

He lifted my head to face him. "Look at me." I looked into his eyes "I know you didn't know, Mari. It's OK."

"What's OK?" I said indignantly. "My best friend professes his love for me not even a month after I bury my husband, who was also his friend?"

Aaron sighed and looked in the direction of Jax. "I knew it when he first described you to me. I could tell in his voice that there was something more than friendly love he had for you. But I was selfish. When I met you, I wanted you for myself. I can't be selfish anymore."

"What are you saying to me, Aaron? I loved *you*. I will *always* love you." He looked at me with those honey brown eyes, and then I woke up.

After my dream, I prayed and prayed for clarity and for answers. I asked the Lord to reveal to me what all of these dreams, Jax's confession, and seeing Aaron meant. As I prayed, I heard in my spirit, *Go to the garden.* I did as my spirit guided and walked out to the garden. There again was Aaron standing at the oak tree. I couldn't help but think that this was just another dream, but I was wide awake, and I knew it wasn't. Aaron was right in front of me, in our rose garden. He turned to face me.

"Hey my lovely Mariposa."

I smiled. He looked different. His body was translucent. It glowed softly in the moon light. While I looked at him, I thought about asking him about the letters or telling him about my conversation with Jax and about the dream I just had, but I didn't want to miss the opportunity to ask him what I really needed to know.

"Why are you here, Aaron? Why did you come back like this?"

He looked at me, but didn't answer. I stared at him, confused and sad. He touched my face, but it wasn't like in my dream. I wasn't able to feel his touch, only warmth and light from where his hand rested on my skin. I closed my eyes, not knowing what to make of what was happening, but wanting to make the most of what we were sharing at the moment.

"You have to go now, Mari," I heard him say.

"I don't want to go. I want to stay here with you."

"Honey, you have to go have our baby."

He touched my stomach, and it began to glow. I felt the baby move inside of me. I didn't know what he had done, but whatever it was sent me into labor. I looked at him.

"You need to go get Mom now."

As he spoke, I felt a twinge in my stomach and then a pain. I moved slowly into the house. As I moved, I felt a squeezing pain.

"Mama," I called. "I think it's time."

"What?" She came running out of my bedroom. "Where were you? Are you OK?"

"I'm fine Mama. We just need to go."

"Okay, honey, where is your bag?"

I didn't have a bag ready. With all that was going on, I forgot to make one. My mother packed a bag while I called the hospital. After my bag was packed, we headed out of the door. On the way, I called my father and Jax.

"It's time, Jax," I said "Meet us there."

The nurses wheeled me into a room and seven and a half hours later, I delivered a baby girl. I loved her from the moment I laid eyes on her. She was so beautiful and perfect. My mother counted all of her fingers and toes just to make sure. Jax looked on proudly. My little baby girl looked up at me, and as I looked into her eyes, I cried a little. She has eyes like my Aaron, and it was then that I knew that he would always be with me.

"What are you going to name her," Jax asked.

"Well, before Aaron went overseas, we discussed naming the baby after him if it was a boy and naming it after me if it was a girl, but I think that I'm going to name her after both of us.

"So what's the name going to be?"

"Erin Mari-Emmanuelle Trent"

"It's beautiful. And I know Aaron would be proud, because he gets to give the baby three names," Jax chuckled.

I giggled a little as I held my baby close to me. I marveled at how all of the events had happened in such a short amount of time. I had to thank God for bringing me through, and I said a little prayer asking Him to continue to lead me in the right direction because I certainly needed help.

After they sent me home, I stayed in the house. I didn't venture out to the rose garden. Also, the dreams had stopped. I had Erin, and my mother stuck around to help me take care of her for the first few weeks.

I barely had time to think about Aaron, but at night when everything and everyone was quiet, I found myself wanting to go out to the garden to see if what I had experienced was real or just God's way of helping me deal with the loss of my one and only love. One particular night I decided to make sure.

I walked into the garden at midnight, hoping I would see Aaron again. He was waiting for me. He smiled when he saw me with the baby.

"I missed you. What took you so long to come back?"

"I *did* have our baby," I giggled. "Also, honestly, I wasn't sure if this was real. If *you* were real."

"I understand," he said with his head down. He slowly looked up. "She's beautiful. What is her name?"

"Erin Mari-Emanuelle," I said smiling.

"You gave her my name."

"She's yours, why wouldn't I?

I saw tears well up in Aaron's eyes. "I wish I could hold her."

I took her close to him. "I know you can't hold her, but you can give her a kiss."

Aaron came close to the baby and gently kissed her forehead. Erin's face illuminated as his lips touched her, and the tears he let drop on her face looked like stars shining in the sky glowing as they streamed down into her blanket. She squirmed a bit, rubbing her eyes and yawning, almost waking.

"She has your eyes," I told him. "You can't see them now, but they are exactly like yours."

His smile made his already brilliant face brighter. It made me want to stay in that moment forever. Aaron's bright smile and our baby girl…our family. I didn't want the night to end, but I knew it had to. I looked at him and asked one more time.

"Why did you come, Aaron?"

"He said you needed me, so He sent me."

I looked at him and sighed. "I will always need you."

"Then I will always be here. Every Spring, as long as you need me I will be here."

"Is that a promise?" I asked.

Aaron smiled. He stepped back from me and Erin toward the oak tree and bowed his head.

"Is that a promise?" I repeated

"I love you, Sophia Marie, and I always will. As long as you need me, I will be here."

And then he was gone. I hugged Erin close to me and went back into the house. When morning came, I didn't tell my mother about my last dream before the baby was born or about seeing Aaron, *really seeing Aaron. Twice.* That piece of information I chose to keep to myself. I did, however, tell her about my conversation with Jax. All she said was God's will be done. I really couldn't be mad at that. I mean that's all I've ever wanted for my life, and now I wanted it for my baby. I thought and prayed a lot about everything, especially the last dream I had about Aaron. I really didn't know if dreaming about Aaron and seeing him were his way of letting me know it was ok to love again or what. I still didn't truly understand why God sent my Aaron back to me the way He did, but I was glad for it. And I couldn't wait for the next spring to arrive.

Summer Secrets & Sins

The Hope & Bliss Story: Part 2

By Janell

"I'm here to pick up a wedding dress. Last name is Hope."

The fifty-something year old seamstress with a heavy Jamaican accent peered up from the evening gown she was altering and smiled at the recognition of the familiar face.

"Yes, yes, Victoria! It's ready! I'll go get it. You are going to be a beautiful bride!" the woman exclaimed before rushing to the rear of the store and disappearing into a back room.

"Actually, I'm . . .," the customer began to say, but the seamstress was already out-of-sight. Instead of finishing her response, a heavy sigh escaped her lips. She began to proceed toward the store's register when a sharp buzzing in her purse halted her. Opening the purse, she jostled its contents around as she searched for the source of the sound and retrieved a cell phone a few seconds later.

"Hello," she said, after pressing the answer button and holding the phone up to her ear. "I'm here now . . . I'll stop by and drop it off in about an hour . . . Okay, see you then."

Being distracted by the call, the customer did not hear the sound of another in the store, did not see the suspicious figure quickly approach her, and did not feel the sharp pinch of the drug-filled needle until it was too late.

Several minutes later, the seamstress reappeared. "I just finished it yesterday," she began, but paused upon noticing the empty store.

"Victoria?" she called out, but no one responded. "Hmm," she murmured as she hung the wedding dress up on a nearby rack and returned to the evening gown she had been working on. "Americans. So impatient."

***

Victoria unloaded a small box from Byron's truck and dropped it on the floor in the far right corner of the living room of his loft. "That's the last one," she said before walking over to the oversized olive-colored sofa and plopping down on it.

Byron looked at her, smiled, and walked over to the same sofa, sitting down next to her. "Wow. This is really happening. We're really getting married in three days."

"Don't sound so excited," Victoria said.

"Babe, you know I'm excited about spending the rest of my life with you. I just can't believe that the day is almost here. On Monday, July 4, you will be Mrs. Byron Bliss."

"Excuse me? I will be Dr. Victoria Hope-Bliss. I'm keeping my name. I've worked too hard to give it up for some smooth-talking player!"

He grinned. "Oh, really? Come here and let me show you just how smooth-talking this player can be." He wrapped his left arm around her shoulders and attempted to pull her in for a kiss. She put her hands over her face to block the attempt, causing him to use his right hand to free her lips.

She laughed at their childlike tussle. "Stop, Byron! You're going to mess up my hair and then everyone at the bridal shower is going to think we were fooling around."

He shrugged, still trying to make his way toward her lips. "So. And maybe we were fooling around. We are about to be married anyways so . . ."

Vicki stood up quickly. "So, whatever. Don't get weak on me now. We only have four more days, and we can give up this abstinence vow and do whatever we want, whenever we want to, however we want to."

"Mm. I like when you talk dirty like that." He hungrily looked at his future bride for a few moments then accepted defeat. "OK, four more days and, woman, you don't even know!"

Vicki kissed him on the forehead. "I'm not worried about you. But who I am worried about is Vivian. She was supposed to pick up my dress from the seamstress and bring it to me a couple of hours ago, but I haven't heard from her, and she's not answering her phone."

"Babe, don't stress. She probably just got caught up and is planning to bring it to the shower tonight. Everything is going to be fine."

"I don't know, Byron. Viv is my identical twin, and twins have this thing, kind of like ESP. We know when something is not right with the other one, and I can sense that something isn't right with her."

"I know that this is an emotional time for the both of us, but we've got to stay calm. Hopefully, she will be at the shower when you get there." Byron looked at his watch and sighed. "I need to get going. Tonight, I've got one more night class to teach before the wedding. Dr. Lawson will fill-in for me while I am off for two weeks, but I've got to go back in again tomorrow afternoon to meet with several students for a class project. Now I'm regretting signing up for summer courses. I should have been like you and taken the summer off. Oh well." He looked up at his bride who wore a defeated expression.

Byron stood up and pulled her into his embrace. "Vicki, look at me. Everything is going to work out. Vivian is OK, and this is going to be one of the happiest moments of our lives. God brought us together and now He is allowing us to become man and wife. No devil in Hell can stop this wedding."

***

Vivian stirred from her unconscious state. When her eyes regained their focus, she found herself bound hand and foot to a wooden chair, which was tied to a metal pole in the basement of someone's house. At first, she thought she was dreaming until she pulled against the rope around her wrist and felt the very real burn of the twine tugging on her skin. She tried to yell out for help, but the silver colored duct tape over her mouth muffled the sound. *Oh my! I've been abducted!* she thought once she realized getting away would not be easy.

In her mind, she tried to replay her most recent memories to make sense out of her situation. She remembered going to pick up her sister's wedding dress, the seamstress going to the back of the store to get the dress, Vicki calling her about dropping off the dress, and then . . . a sharp pain in her neck and the image of a familiar face before everything faded into black.

She found relief in knowing that Vicki would sense her distress. As twins, they had an uncanny way of perceiving the other's feelings. She was certain that her sister would not rest until she found her. She only hoped two things: one, her kidnapping wouldn't interfere with Vicki's wedding and two, Vicki would find her still alive.

***

Vicki arrived at her bridal shower at 7 PM. To her dismay, Vivian was not there. Anxious, but wanting to maintain control, she continued with the evening's activities until she could no longer contain her emotions, which occurred when the clock struck 8 o'clock, and Vivian was still unaccounted for.

Bursting into tears, Vicki ran out of the living room of her soon-to-be-rented house and into the kitchen. Aunt Mabel, who was at the time cutting herself a piece of the cake that had not yet been presented to the bride, looked up at her niece, licked white frosting off of her index finger, and said, "Whatchu crying for?"

Vicki hesitated briefly before opening up to her aunt. Mabel wasn't high on her list of people to confide in, but she was an expert at was being nosey which Vicki needed at the moment. If there was a mystery to be solved, Aunt Mabel was the perfect snoop to put on the case. "Vivian is missing! She was supposed to drop off my wedding dress, and she never showed up. My sister would never miss my bridal shower, so the fact that she's not here tells me that something is horribly wrong. She's not answering her cell phone, and her husband

David says she isn't at home. What if something really, really bad happened to her? I can't get married without her by my side!"

Mabel eyed the unopened bag of plastic forks. "Calm yourself, child. You 'bout to work yourself into a tizzy, and the girl ain't been gone longer than a few hours. No tellin' where she might be," Mabel said before ripping the bag open, touching almost all of the forks with her unwashed hands, and pulling one out for her own use.

Victoria shuttered at the thought of using any of the remaining forks. Luckily, she wasn't in the eating mood. "Aunt Mabel, something is wrong. She is in trouble; I can feel it. Can you help me look for her? I have to find her, or there won't be a wedding on Monday. There is no way that I can marry Byron and go on our honeymoon, knowing that my own sister is out there suffering."

Mabel ate a chunk of the vanilla-frosted, yellow cake before responding. "I really ain't got time for this mess, but I'ma help you 'cause if you let this man go, you might never find another man to put up with your uppity self. You're already getting old, and you probably only have a few good eggs left, so for the sake of my late sister, God rest her soul, I'll help you look for Vivian tomorrow."

"But we need to—"

"Tomorrow. Ain't nothing we can do now; it's almost 9 o'clock at night. By the morning, if she never comes home, we'll know she's really missing. Now let's finish up this bridal shower so I can go home and soak my feet." Mabel waved Vicki away. "Go on and open your presents and cut your cake."

Vicki rolled her eyes. "But you already cut my cake."

Mabel licked her fork and began to dig back into the disappearing piece of cake on her plate. "Y'all was taking too long. You can cut the second piece. Go on out there with your guests and leave me alone."

At 9 o'clock sharp, Vicki banged urgently on Aunt Mabel's front door. Byron stood back, away from the door, covering his face and shaking his head in disapproval. After a few minutes of Vicki's annoying, consistent knocking, Aunt Mabel jerked the door open with one hand and swung a wooden bat at the entryway with the other. If Vicki had not jumped back and ducked, she would have found herself laid out on the ground, black and blue from being cracked upside the head by the bat.

"What in the devil is wrong with you? Banging on my door this early in the morning like you're the sheriff," Aunt Mabel grumbled after leaning the bat against the wall inside the house.

"You'd better be glad I wasn't the sheriff. If I had been, you'd be going to jail for assault with a deadly weapon." Vicki pouted and walked into the house. She entered the living room and sat down on the sofa without so much as a hello or invitation to come in.

Byron also stepped into the house, but said, "Good morning, Aunt Mabel," before joining his fiancée on the sofa.

Vicki looked over at him and noticing his judgmental expression said, "What?"

He shook his head again. "Nothing. We're here now, so tell us the plan."

"What plan?" Mabel asked, pulling her terry cloth robe tighter around her.

"Viv is still missing. I talked to David this morning, and she didn't return home last night. He called the police, but we all know that they won't file a missing persons report for three days. We don't have three days to wait so we're going to have to handle the case ourselves. David is already out, talking with her friends and coworkers. I say, we retrace her steps and look for clues."

Mabel snickered. "So who are you, now? CSI?"

"What else are we supposed to do? Just sit back and pray she comes home?"

"That's a start. I vote for that plan."

"Aunt Mabel!"

"Calm down, girl. Don't annoy me before I've had my morning cup of coffee. I have been known to go off and call you every name but a child of God. I'm agoing in this here kitchen and pour me a cup. By the time I come back, I'll tell you what we're gonna do."

Mabel exited the room and Vicki huffed in frustration. "She's impossible. Lord, what are we going to do?"

Byron scooted closer to his future wife and wrapped his left arm around her shoulder, rubbing it comfortingly. "Babe, I know you're upset, but you have to chill out. Panicking isn't going to solve the problem. We have to be calm so we can think rationally about this matter. We're going to figure it out; I know we will. I love you, and in three days, we are going to get married, and your sister will be there."

"Byron . . . I can't marry you if we don't find my sister."

"What?" Byron's eyes widened.

"I can't. How can I make the most important decision in my life without my sister with me, especially if something bad has happened to her? Our mother is deceased, our father is who knows where, and my half-brother along with the rest of my family is crazy. I can't do this without her," Vicki sobbed.

"I understand, babe, but we can't stop the wedding. Everything is already paid for, our guests are in town; we can't throw it all away over one person."

"Obviously, you don't understand. And we're not talking about just one person; we're talking about my other half."

"I'm supposed to be your other half!" Byron said, clearly upset.

Mabel entered into the living room with a hot mug of coffee in her hand. "What are y'all fussing about in here? Law'd it's too early to have folks carrying on in my house. Y'all gonna have to get out."

"Aunt Mabel!" Vicki shrieked.

Mabel rolled her eyes and sat down on an oversized recliner. "Okay, okay. Y'all can stay until I finish drinking my coffee, but then y'all got to go. And since that means you only got a few minutes, let me tell you what we need to do. We either need to first figure out if she's been in some kind of accident.

"Before we came here, I called all of the hospitals, and David told me he has called the police. Nobody's reported anything and she is not listed as a patient at any of the hospitals." Vicki unconsciously played with her engagement band. "It seems highly unlikely that she was in an accident. It's worst. I can sense it. Someone did something awful to her."

Mabel blew on the brown liquid in her mug. "Then we need to establish a motive."

"A motive?" Byron asked.

"All those investigation TV shows I watch, they all point out the motive. Once you figure out why someone would snatch Vivian up, it will help you know where to look for her."

Byron nodded. "That's smart, Aunt Mabel. But who would have a problem with Vivian? She's one of the sweetest people I know."

Mabel sipped her coffee. "Who knows? But y'all should start thinking about the why."

"It doesn't make sense. Vivian has always been the peacemaker. I can't think of a single soul who would want to hurt her. If anyone, I was the one out of the two of us who has always been disliked," Vicki said.

Mabel sipped her coffee again. "Well, maybe that's it. Maybe you're the reason she is missing."

"Okay, so why not hurt me and not her?"

"You two are twins," Mabel said. "It wouldn't be the first time that someone mistook Vivian for you."

"It still doesn't add up. Even if someone was out to get me, why would they hurt or even kidnap me or Vivian? It's not like they could get a large ransom for either of us. I still think that we need to head over to the seamstress' place. That was the last place that I know she was at before she disappeared."

Mabel placed her mug down on the coffee table in front of her. "Y'all go do that."

"Aren't you coming? You said you would help me find her."

"Do I have to do everything?" Mabel threw her hands up. "Law'd, this girl about to drive me crazy. All right, let me go put my good wig on."

The bells on the door chimed as Vicki entered through the glass door of the seamstress' boutique. Byron and Aunt Mabel decided to wait in the car in an effort not to alarm the easily excitable woman. The moment she spotted Victoria, she ran up to her and grabbed her hands, shaking them anxiously. "Ahh! Miss Victoria. You're back. I knew you'd be back. The dress is so beautiful; you had to come back."

Vicki felt confused. "What?"

"I went to get your dress, and I came back and you were gone." The seamstress waived her hands frantically as she spoke.

"Huh?"

The seamstress pointed at a rack. "Your dress. Yesterday, you came to pick it up, but you left. I hung it over here because I knew you'd be back."

"But . . . I didn't come here yesterday."

"Yes, you did. I saw you."

Vicki shook her head. "Oh, no. My sister Vivian came to pick up the dress. We're twins. She is who you saw. . . But what? I—she left? Are you saying that she didn't get the dress when she was here?"

"No! That's what I'm trying to tell you. I thought it was you. I went to get the dress, and when I came back, nobody was here." She looked over at the dress, still hanging nearby. "Do you want it now?"

Vicki felt her heart drop in fear. "I guess . . . I mean . . . sure."

The seamstress looked Vicki skeptically, shook her head, and spoke aloud as if she couldn't be seen or heard by her customer. "Mm. Crazy child. Weddings make smart women foolish."

When Vicki exited the boutique several minutes later, Byron and Aunt Mabel were in the parking lot, leaning against Byron's SUV.

"Is that your wedding dress?" Byron asked as he noticed Vicki load a large garment bag into the truck's hatchback.

Vicki slammed the rear door shut. "Yes, and you're not supposed to see it."

Byron frowned. "Why do *you* have it? I thought Vivian picked it up."

Vicki joined them, leaning against the truck closest to Byron. "Me too. The seamstress says she came to get it, but disappeared before she could take the dress. Byron, I'm really, really concerned now. She wouldn't have left without the dress. Something is definitely wrong."

He scratched his head. "Did she say anything else about Vivian?"

"No. Only that Vivian was gone. I feel like we've reached a dead end."

Aunt Mabel stepped away from the truck and placed her right hand on her hip. "I told y'all to come up with a motive. Obviously, something happened between her going in that store and the seamstress coming out with the dress. To figure out what happened, you gotta first figure out why it happened."

Vicki nodded. "OK, Aunt Mabel. You're probably right. So why would someone want to hurt Vivian?"

"Or why would someone want to hurt you?" Mabel asked.

"Huh?"

Mabel pointed at Vicki with her index finger. "You said yourself that everyone likes Vivian, but people don't always like you. And, might I add, you're getting married in a few days. I don't know child; maybe someone wanted to keep you from getting married. Maybe they got Vivian because they knew it would hurt you."

Vicki gasped. "Or maybe they thought Vivian was me."

Byron looked back and forth between the two women. "Babe, do you really think someone mistook Vivian for you?"

"The seamstress said that she thought Viv was me. You guys said it earlier too, that people have mistook us for each other in the past. Someone else could have also made the same mistake."

Mabel pulled a peppermint out of her purse and began to unwrap it. "Either way, you need to start counting your enemies."

Vicki pouted. "My mind is blank. I know there are people who don't care much for me, but I can't come up with anyone who would kidnap me or my sister."

Byron looked at his watch. "Babe, I hate to run out on you right now, but I need to go up to the campus for a little while. Are you and Aunt Mabel going to be okay?"

Vicki pushed her body away from the truck. "Yes, because we're going with you. While you're working Aunt Mabel and I can brainstorm. If someone is out to get me, I don't want to be vulnerable by sitting at home alone. Plus, we can't stop digging until we find her."

Vicki and Byron both looked at Aunt Mabel as if they expected her to resist. Mabel popped the unwrapped peppermint into her mouth, tossed the plastic wrapper onto the ground, rolled her eyes at the both of them, and proceeded to climb back into the truck.

"I can't stand that little girl," Victoria said in annoyance as she watched one of Byron's students swoon over him. Vicki and Mabel sat in club chairs in the library approximately twenty feet away from Byron. He was seated at a large, wooden table, surrounded by several of his summer school students.

"Who is that?" Mabel asked.

"Trina or Tina or Trisha . . . I can't remember her name. She's one of his fast-tailed students who's in love with him. I swear I think that child purposely flunked his class and didn't graduate on time just to be able to be near him. Look at her over there. She can't keep her hands off of him. When did these young girls become so flirtatious?"

"I seem to remember that you too used to be 'flirtatious.' I used to have to beat you like you stole something just to keep you away from those boys."

Vicki laughed. "Stop exaggerating. I was never that bad. I went to the prom with one boy, and you were convinced that I was the hottest thing on the block." Vicki eyed a woman walking into the library. "Is that Nancy?" she said to Mabel who shrugged her shoulders. "It is. Nancy! Nancy! Come here," she whispered loudly.

Nancy, being spotted, left out a heavy sigh and approached the table where Vicki and Mabel sat. She appeared worn out and tired, and the smile she gave the women was far from authentic. "Victoria," she said without emotion.

Vicki ignored her friend's cold greeting. "Hey! Where have you been? I've called you a zillion times. Haven't you gotten my messages?"

"Oh . . . yeah. I'm sorry, my phone has been acting up and things have been really busy lately with me teaching summer school and teaching online classes too."

"I can imagine. Oh, excuse me. You remember my Aunt Mabel, right?"

Nancy quickly glanced in Mabel's direction and nodded. "Yes. Hello, Aunt Mabel. How are you?"

Mabel grunted. "I'd be better if I was at home watching my soaps, but I'm all right, I guess."

Vicki cleared her throat. "Nancy, you know the wedding is on July 4, this Monday. I never got your RSVP. Were you planning to come?"

Nancy briefly looked at Byron, who was still surrounded by students, and then refocused her attention back to Vicki. "I–I totally forgot. If I can pull myself from under all of this grading, I'll try to make it. Listen, sorry to run, but I've got to be somewhere like now, so I'll catch you later, okay?"

"Sure. Bye." Vicki watched Nancy rapidly depart from the table and head to the second floor of the library. "That was weird. You know, she's been acting funny lately. We used to be so close, and now it's like she doesn't make time for me anymore. I mean, how could she forget that I was getting married? She was one of the people who wanted me to give Byron a chance, but once he and I started dating, she . . ."

"She became jealous. There is your motive. Nancy is Suspect #1," Mabel said, matter-of-factly.

Vicki shook her head. "What? No, I can't believe she–"

"Believe it. Right now, everyone is a possible suspect. Someone you or Viv knows did this. You can't start ruling people out because you thought they were your friends. And the way that woman just treated you like you were gum on the bottom of her shoe, yeah, she definitely could have done the crime."

Vicki placed the palm of her hand on her forehead. "Oh my gosh. I never really thought about the people around me, that they would try to hurt me like this. This changes everything."

"I bet it does. It's time for you to stop playing CSI and figure this thing out because I need a nap. Got me all running around town, and you still haven't come up with suspects. That's it. Who in your life might want to stop this wedding? Tell me now before I call me a cab and leave you and your man to figure this out on your own."

"Sorry, Aunt Mabel. This is really hard for me. OK, let me think. Uh . . . well there's my ex-boyfriend, Scott. He's called me a bunch of times trying to get back together and claiming I'm marrying the wrong man. He definitely doesn't want to see me married."

Aunt Mabel offered half of a smile. "Now we're getting somewhere. Scott is Suspect #2. You better start writing all of this down. Who else?"

"I don't know. All of my friends are in the wedding or coming to it. I don't really hang around anyone else but the family and the only person in the family I can tell doesn't seem to be happy about me getting married is Katrina."

"Who?"

"Katrina. My brother's wife. The one whose cooking you always complain about."

Mabel chuckled. "Oh yeah. I thought her name was Ka-tastrophe."

"Aunt Mabel."

"Unless you are Jesus, stop calling my name. That girl is a catastrophe, old non-cooking self. Well, let's add her to the list. She's Suspect #3." Mabel stood up from the table. "It's time that you paid a visit to each of your suspects, but before you do that, take me home."

Vicki decided to borrow Byron's truck, drop Mabel off, and confront the one person she really felt could try to ruin her wedding, her ex-boyfriend Scott. Parking in front of Scott's three story home, Vicki took a deep breath, searching for the guts to accuse Scott of something so outrageous. She was aware that he'd never admit it even if he had something to do with Viv's disappearance. She would have to be slick with her approach if she wanted to get any information out of him at all.

Still unsure of what to say, she exited the SUV, walked up to the front door, and rang the bell. A minute later, Scott opened the door, grinning confidently at the sight of Vicki.

"I figured you'd show up," he said as he leaned against the door jam.

Internally, Vicki wanted to slap him, but she had to play it cool. "Oh really? Why is that?"

"Because I have something you can't live without."

"And what would that be?"

He licked his lips confidently. "You tell me. Why are you here?"

Vicki felt she was getting nowhere. Not knowing what else to say, she replied, "Uh . . . I was wondering if you've seen my sister."

He shifted from one foot to the other, still leaning against the door's frame. "Your sister? I've never met your sister. Remember, you wouldn't let me meet your family."

"I know, but she looks just like me; we're twins. Have you seen someone who looks like me lately?"

He stood upright and moved closer to her. "Victoria, come on and just be honest. You mean to tell me that you came all the way over to my house to ask me if I've seen your sister that you wouldn't let me meet? Not to mention that you're doing this a few days before your *wedding* to that loser. If you want me back, just tell me, and I'll forgive you."

As much as Vicki wanted to remain calm, at that moment she realized how much she disliked Scott and herself for ever dating him. "Forgive me? You're the one that cheated. I love Byron, and even if he and I weren't getting married, I would never, ever, ever-ever-ever-ever want you back."

Vicki screamed in frustration and stomped back to the SUV. Talking to Scott was futile and aggravating. If he was involved in Vivian's disappearance, he wasn't going to make it easy for her to get a confession.

Before heading back to pick up Byron, Vicki made one last stop at Katrina's job. Katrina worked four days a week (Wednesdays through Saturdays) as an Executive Administrative Assistant for Kodak. Victoria had visited Katrina several times in the past, so getting past security wasn't difficult. She rode the elevator to Katrina's floor, trying to conjure up a plan to get Katrina talking, but their love-hate relationship would surely act as a barrier.

Saying a quick, mental prayer, Vicki strolled into Katrina's office as if she was a co-worker and sat down in one of the plastic and metal chairs stationed in front of her desk. "Good afternoon, Katrina."

"Vicki? What are you doing here?" Katrina snapped.

"Just trying to get things in order for my wedding. Are you coming to the bachelorette party tomorrow night?"

"I didn't know I was invited."

Vicki plastered on a fake smile. "Of course you are! Didn't Vivian tell you? Oh, well maybe Viv didn't get a chance yet since she's been MIA since yesterday. But I'm sure she'll surface soon. You know Viv."

Katrina shifted in her seat. "So, is that why you're here?"

"Is what why I'm here?" Vicki held her breath, hoping Katrina would give her some information that she could work with.

"To see if I'm coming to your party?"

Vicki exhaled in disappointment. "Yeah, I mean you missed the bridal shower so I figured I would check on you."

"Aren't you so considerate? I'm fine; I just had other things to do yesterday."

"Like what?" Vicki said, slightly annoyed. "What could be more important than the bridal shower of your sister-in-law?"

Katrina winced and said in a barely audible voice, "I had something I had to pick up."

Vicki noticed a slight change in demeanor. She couldn't pinpoint whether Katrina was hiding something or just being her usual difficult self. "Really? Like my wedding gift or an unexpected relative?"

Katrina sprang up from her chair and moved from behind her desk to her office door. "Like none of your business. I'm at work, and right now isn't a good time. I would appreciate if you called first before just popping in. If it's that important to you, I'll come to the bachelorette party, okay? Now, please leave," she said as she waved her hand in front of the door, signaling that Vicki's visit was over.

Feeling exhausted from playing Agatha Christie all day long and irritated by her sister-in-law's nice-nasty attitude, Vicki stood up from the chair and headed out the door. "No problem. See you tomorrow."

In the car an hour later, Vicki filled Byron in on the list of suspects and her unsuccessful attempts at being a detective. She noticed that he seemed to stiffen up at the idea of her dropping by her ex-boyfriend's house, but he never complained. After dishing out all of the details,

Vicki rested her head against the black, leather seat and sighed heavily. "I'm so frustrated and scared," she admitted.

Byron steered the truck into the parking garage connected to his (and soon-to-be her) loft's building. After putting the vehicle into park, he reached over and rubbed his fiancée's knee. "I know you are. I am so sorry you have to go through this, that we have to go through this. Let's just pray that Vivian is safe and that we will be able to find her in time for the wedding. I wish I had the answers, but at least I know the One who does."

Victoria meekly nodded her head, and right there inside the SUV in the parking garage, the couple began to pray for their missing loved one.

***

Vivian had been left alone for the majority of the day with her thoughts. To keep herself from going insane, she prayed and recited Psalm 23 over and over again in her mind. She couldn't believe that she had been kidnapped, and even more so, she couldn't believe the person who had outwitted her. She would have never thought someone who appeared so normal would have the mentality to orchestrate something so evil.

She heard the footsteps of her attacker as the person walked down the basement stairs and came up close to her. Without regard for her, the assailant reached over and ripped the duct tape away from her mouth, causing her to scream out in pain.

"Shut up or you won't eat!"

Vivian choked back her tears and muffled her cry. She was parched and hungry, so her pain would have to take a backseat. The enemy fed her soup, bread, and bottled water. Although the meal wasn't the tastiest, Vivian was grateful for anything that would silence the hunger pains and growing dehydration.

Upon finishing the feeding, the aggressor replaced the old duct tape with fresh tape. Looking down at Vivian with disgust, the person said, "I'm sorry that I had to do this to you. It wasn't supposed to be you. Victoria should have been the one sitting in this basement, tied up like the dog she truly is! I thought you were her; you two look so much a like even down to the way you both wear your hair. Well, the good thing is that even though I snatched the wrong woman, my plan is still working. She won't be able to marry Byron with her poor, twin sister missing. Unfortunately for you, once this is all over, I'm going to have to kill you. You know who I am, and I can't take the chance of you ratting me out. Just know that it's nothing personal."

***

Sunday morning was melancholic. Vicki and Byron sat in the center section, fifth row in the sanctuary at Greater Mercy Pentecostal Church. No word had still been heard from or about Vivian, and both Vicki and David were emotional wrecks. David sat next to the couple in church seemingly lost without his spouse. When the hymn "God Will Take Care of You" was sung by the congregation, Vicki took

David's hand into her own and squeezed it comfortingly. Even Pastor Thomas seemed to be in the same mindset when he delivered a powerful sermon entitled "Leaning on the Everlasting Arms."

After the service, Vicki, Byron, and David stood huddled in the parking lot of the church, mulling over the past two days and Viv's disappearance. David had spoken to everyone Viv knew from friends to coworkers to neighbors, but no one had seen or heard from her. Although Vicki hated the idea that Nancy, Katrina, or even Scott could have been involved in Viv's disappearance, she somewhat hoped it was one of them. If all of them were ruled out as the culprit, she would be clueless of where to look next.

Just as the crew was planning to head towards their cars, Aunt Mabel penetrated the small group, big church hat, white stockings and all. "Whatch'all over her yapping about? Vivian?"

"Of course, Aunt Mabel. What else is there to talk about right now?" Vicki said.

Byron gave Vicki a cross expression, but he did not speak.

"Hm," Mabel grunted. "Well, Sister Jenkins said that she saw Ka-tastrophe on Friday afternoon at the Walmart close to that bridal shop looking all suspicious and acting like she didn't want to be seen. She said she waved at the girl, and Ka-tastrophe had the nerve to look her dead in her eyes and keep walking without a word."

"Who is Catastrophe?" Byron asked.

"Aunt Mabel thinks Katrina's name is Ka-tastrophe," Vicki answered.

"I've called that child Ka-tastrophe to her face."

Vicki laughed. "I bet you did."

"So Aunt Mabel, you think Katrina is the one that took Vivian?" Byron asked.

"I said no such thing. I am just telling y'all what I heard. What y'all do with the information is up to y'all." She turned her attention toward Vicki. "But if you plan to figure out who snatched Viv, you better start asking Ms. Thing some questions."

Vicki exhaled and nodded. "When I see her tonight at the bachelorette party, I'll confront her about it."

Byron and Vicki returned to the church later that afternoon for the rehearsal, but with the absence of Vivian, the activity was cut short. It had also been decided in advance that they would forgo the rehearsal dinner, and allow Byron and Vicki to instead enjoy their separate bachelor and bachelorette parties. With the wedding falling on a Monday, and Vicki not being the clubbing type, it was decided that her bachelorette party would be held that Sunday night at a high-end hotel, and would consist of a catered meal, virgin frozen drinks, and throwback party games like Pictionary and Truth or Dare. Byron would hold his bachelor's party simultaneously at the loft, and both parties would end by midnight so that the couple and their guests could get adequate rest and preparation time for their July 4th, 4 P.M. wedding.

With Vivian, the matron-of-honor, missing, the other bridesmaids had to fill in with helping to organize and run the bachelorette party. Several of the bridesmaids and guests asked about Vivian's whereabouts, but Vicki, unsure of who had committed the sin against her, kept Viv's vanishing a secret and only said that Vivian was tied up for the moment.

To Vicki's satisfaction, Katrina did make it to the party, but continued to behave strange and distant. Despite the fact that it was the middle of summer and at least 80 degrees outside even at night, Katrina wore a long sleeved turtleneck and a pair of jeans. She kept her arms folded and tried to be as inconspicuous as possible, which for Victoria, made her look guiltier.

By the time the game Truth of Dare was in motion, Vicki was bursting at the seams to challenge Katrina. To avoid being obvious, Vicki waited until it was her second chance to pick someone before selecting Katrina.

"Truth or dare, Katrina?" Vicki knew Katrina would never pick dare, and if she did, Vicki would torture her for it.

"Truth."

Vicki smiled. "Katrina, is it true that you're trying to sabotage my wedding?"

"What? No!" Katrina shrieked.

The other women at the party gasped in surprise and looked back and forth between Victoria and Katrina. "Where's Vivian?"

"I don't know. I thought you said she was tied up."

"Why don't you tell me, is she?"

"Huh?"

"Stop playing games. Where were you on Friday? Someone saw you at Walmart on Chili Avenue."

"I told you that I was picking something up."

"What? My sister?"

"What are you talking about?"

"Don't play coy with me. Why have you been acting so funny lately? Why do you have a turtleneck on when it's a zillion degrees outside? And what were you 'picking up' on Friday that caused you to miss my bridal shower?"

"A prescription for allergy medicine!"

"Yeah, right."

Katrina sighed. "If you must know, your brother came home on Thursday with some kind of massage oil for married couples, claiming he wanted us to spice things up in the bedroom by giving each other sensual massages. I don't know what the stuff was made out of, but by the next morning, I was covered in hives. I had to take the day off from work on Friday and was medicated for the rest of the day after I picked up my prescription. That's why I missed your party. When you came by the office yesterday, I was behind on my work from the previous day so I didn't have time to fool around with you. And I have on a turtleneck now because my skin is all blotchy and I didn't want people looking at me funny." Katrina grabbed the collar of the turtleneck and pulled it down a bit, exposing her neck and irritated skin.

The room became awkwardly silent and all eyes fell on Vicki for a response. "Oh."

Feeling defeated, Vicki left the bachelorette party an hour early. Suspect #3, Katrina, was dead end. That only left Scott and Nancy, and the wedding was rapidly approaching. Out of the two, if she was a betting woman, she would bet on Scott. The day prior he told her that he had something she couldn't live without. Yes, she had never introduced him to Vivian, but she constantly spoke about her to him and he had seen pictures of the twins before. It had to be Scott.

Desperate, she raced back over to Scott's house, determined to find her sister. It was 11:20 PM by the time she pulled into his driveway, but Vicki didn't care about the time. She rushed to his door and rang the bell several times in a row. After a couple of minutes, she could hear his footsteps as he approached the door.

"Who is it?" he yelled angrily through the metal door without a peephole.

"It's Victoria."

"Victoria?" He unlocked and opened the door, appearing as if he had been pulled away from a deep slumber. "Girl, what you doin' here so late?"

"What do you think?"

"Oh." He grinned. "So, you changed your mind?"

"No. I'm here for my sister."

"What is it with you and this sister thing?"

"You said that you have something that I can't live without. What do you have that I can't live without?"

He licked his lips seductively. "Your heart. I've got your heart."

"Eww." Vicki turned up her face in disgust at the thought. "Man, move." Vicki was tired of the verbal dance with Scott. She needed to see for herself if he was indeed the one who had Vivian. She pushed passed him and entered into his house, rummaging through it from room to room despite his objections.

"Viv, you here? Vivian?" she yelled as she scoured the place.

He followed her. "What are you doing? Your sister isn't here."

Vicki spun around to face him. "Then you should have no problem with me searching your house, right?"

"Yes, I have a problem with you searching my house. Who do you think you are?"

"Someone with nothing to hide. Do you have something to hide?"

"No."

"Then let me see for myself."

Scott stopped protesting and allowed Vicki to search the entire house, except for the basement. Once Vicki had looked in every room, Scott asked, "Are you happy?"

"No," Vicki said coolly. "Where's your basement door?"

Scott shook his head. "What? You're not going down in my basement."

"Why not?"

"Because it's a mess. There's no light down there, and if you fall and hurt yourself, you'll be trying to sue me."

"I won't sue you. I'm sure you have a flashlight somewhere around here. Give me the light, I will quickly and carefully check out the basement, and if what you say is true, that Vivian's not down there, I'll leave you alone and let you go back to bed."

Scott grumbled, went into the kitchen and came back into the hallway with a flashlight. He directed her to a door off the hallway, opened it and said, "Hurry up."

Vivian took the flashlight, turned it on, and proceeded to walk down the basement stairs. She knew what she was doing was crazy, that if Scott really had her sister bound and gagged down in his basement, by going down there alone, she would probably also end up in the same position next. But for Victoria, common sense had departed from her mind the moment Vivian disappeared, and she was willing to put her own life on the line for that of her sister's.

The wooden stairs creaked underneath Vicki's feet as she traveled down the last few steps. The basement was pitch-black; the only light came from the medium-sized flashlight in her hand. Victoria aimed the light at the center of the room and then moved it around to scan the entire perimeter. "Vivian!" she called out.

Nothing. There was no response and no sight of her lost sibling.

Disappointed, Vicki climbed the stairs back up to the hallway where Scott waited for her.

"Satisfied?" he asked, smugly.

"Yeah. Thanks," she replied, sadly. "I'm sorry for coming over here so late. I'll go now."

She walked to the door and was about to open it when he caught her by the elbow. "Vicki, you don't have to go. You don't have to marry him. I know I kid around a lot, but seriously, I love you. Can you honestly say that you don't love me anymore?"

Vicki glanced up at him in shock. She was used to the arrogant Scott who had an answer for everything and rarely showed any form of humility or softness. She wasn't used to this Scott who was being gentle and laying his feelings for her out on the line. "Scott, I-I'm sorry. Yes, I still care about you. I guess that's why I get so easily frustrated with you. But I am in love with Byron. My sister is really missing and because of it, I don't know whether or not Byron and I will be getting married in several hours. But regardless if we don't, I won't return to you. That part of my life is over. I think that we both know we're not meant to be."

Vicki tenderly kissed him on the cheek and left his house. Once back in her vehicle, she pulled out her cellphone and dialed Nancy's phone number. It was her last option; both Katrina and Scott had turned out to be innocent. Nancy's phone rang several times before the voicemail picked up. Vicki left a brief message, begging Nancy to call her ASAP. It was too late to drive out to the suburbs where Nancy lived to search her place as she had done with Scott. Flustered, she tossed the phone onto the passenger side seat and steered the car towards Byron's loft.

Having the key, she let herself into the house. Byron was still awake, cleaning up from the seemingly mild bachelor's party. All of the guests had left, and Vicki couldn't help, but wonder why he was stuck with cleaning duty when it was his celebration.

Byron noticed her when she walked into the kitchen and leaned against the counter. "Hey, babe. What are you doing here? I thought you were staying at your place tonight," he said as he began washing dishes.

"I am. I just . . . why are you cleaning? Why isn't someone else doing this?"

"I told them I could handle it and that they could leave. I really wanted some time alone, you know, before tomorrow."

She nodded. "Yeah."

Byron stacked a few recently washed plates on the countertop. "You never said why you were here."

"Katrina and Scott are clean, I think." She went on to tell him about the night's activities. "That only leaves Nancy on our radar. Tomorrow makes seventy-two hours so we can call the police and file a missing persons report. I don't know what else to do."

Byron dried his hands with a yellow dish towel. "You've done all that you can do. Good thing that we are not going on an actual honeymoon. Since we will be here after the wedding, we can use my two weeks off to keep looking for her."

Vicki looked up at him. "I'm sorry, Byron. I'm not marrying you.

He stared down at her with a confused expression. "What do you mean, you aren't marrying me?"

She stood up straight. "I already told you that I can't do this without my sister. We're going to have to postpone the wedding."

He came over to her and lightly grabbed her shoulders. "I can't believe you. We are not postponing the wedding. I will not allow whoever has taken Vivian to ruin our wedding day."

Vicki pushed him away. "And I cannot get married without my best friend."

"You just don't get it, Vicki. You are marrying me, not your sister. I am supposed to be your best friend now, and you're supposed to be mine. You can't just make a decision that affects the both of us without my approval, especially when it has to do with someone else getting in between you and me."

She crossed her arms in front of her chest. "Well I just did. You're going to have to accept that this is who I am. I'm not leaving my sister behind, not for you or anyone else."

He turned his back to her. "Then by default, you're choosing to leave me behind. So tomorrow, when you wake up, you go and tell everyone that the wedding is off. I'm done."

Vicki's eyes filled with tears. "Fine. It's off." She stormed out of the loft, feeling as if at the same time, she was also removing herself from Byron's life.

Victoria awakened to the sound of hard, continuous knocking on her bedroom door. She had locked the door the night prior, wanting some privacy to sort out her feelings about the possibly called-off wedding and her missing sister. With some of her family and friends staying at her place, she didn't want to risk anyone barging in on her.

Wiping the sleep from her eyes, she moaned and yelled out in a groggy voice, "What?"

"Vicki, open the door."

Vicki sat up in the bed. "Byron?"

"Yes, it's me. Open the door."

"But you're not supposed to see me on the wedding day before the ceremony."

"According to you, there won't be a ceremony today, so it shouldn't matter. But that's not the point. I need you to open up the door."

Vicki opened the door, and immediately wrapped her arms around his neck and laid her head on his chest. "Byron, I'm so sorry that I've put you through all of this. You're such a wonderful man, and all you wanted to do was marry me. I just didn't think that I could do this wedding without Viv; I'm so used to her being by my side. I hate to get married without her, but I don't want to lose you in the process. So, if you will still have me, I'd like to marry you today."

Byron entered the room with her still hanging on to him. He closed the door behind them and moved her over to the bed to sit down. "Babe, you will never lose me. I'm here for life. Of course, we can still get married today. But if you want to wait for your sister, we can postpone the wedding. Either way, I want to marry you, Victoria Hope."

"Aww, baby. Let's not wait. I don't think Viv would want us to wait. Let's do it now."

He smiled at her and ran his hand down the side of her face softly. "Okay. You're probably right. Plus, I probably need to be officially taken off the market before one of these female students tries to ambush me."

"What? What are you talking about?"

He shook his head and chucked. "Vicki, you have no idea how crazy some of my students are. I tried not to tell you about it because I didn't want you to get upset, go off on one of them, and risk your job. But they say and do some of the most aggressive things. They try to give me gifts and offer me sex; one even showed up at my loft last night."

Victoria's eyes widened. "Hold on! Who showed up at your place and when?"

"A little while after you left, Trish Patterson showed up. You remember Trish, right? The one you hate who flunked my class in the fall and was retaking it this summer."

"Why was she at your house? How does she even know where you live?"

"I don't know! I thought it was you coming back to apologize, but she was standing on the other side of the door when I opened it."

"Well, what did she want?"

"She was talking crazy. She said something about knowing that I was going through a hard time, but that things would work out in the end. She also mentioned something about wanting to go to Italy or something like that. I had tuned her out by then. I let her talk for a few minutes and then asked her to leave and told her it was inappropriate to come to my house. She—"

Vicki gasped. "Wait! Stop! Go back. You said that she said something about Italy?"

"Yeah, but I don't know—"

"Oh-my-gosh! It's her! Trish is the kidnapper!" Vicki interrupted.

"You think?"

"Yes! It all makes sense now. I know that I told you that I didn't want to go on a real honeymoon and that I wanted to spend two weeks cuddled up here at home, but I was trying to surprise you. My wedding gift to you is a trip to Italy. I gave the plane tickets to Vivian to hide them from you. We were going to surprise you with them at the reception. Vivian put the tickets in her purse for safe keeping. Trish, wanting to stop our wedding, must have abducted her from the boutique, probably thinking that Viv was me. When she went through her purse, she figured out that Viv wasn't me, but she also found the plane tickets, which had your address on them because I switched all of my credit card billings to your place. It's her! I know she has Vivian!"

Byron stood up. "OK, I believe you. I can go online to my classes and pull her address from the database. We can call the police and—"

"No! Without a warrant, the police can't search her place. If we need backup, we need to call Aunt Mabel."

Byron laughed. "What is Aunt Mabel going to do? She's not the law."

"But she thinks she is. I've seen Aunt Mabel handle the biggest of men. Trust me on this one. This is not going to be pretty at all. Vivian knows who Trish is; she saw that picture your class took when they volunteered at that farm out in Avon, and I mentioned to her that the girl had a crush on you. If Trish is crazy enough to kidnap my sister to get to you, no telling what she has done to her. I'll call Mabel, you get the address, and let's go get my sister so that we won't be late to our wedding."

"But, Vicki. What if she denies it or better yet, isn't home. We can't just walk into the woman's house. That's illegal; we could go to jail."

"My sister could be dying. She could be dead already. I don't care about the law right now. If we call the police, they will just question Trish and leave which will give her ample time to dump the evidence. We have to blindside her. This is my sister. Jail time? That's a risk I'm willing to take for someone I love; how about you?

Aunt Mabel, Victoria, and Byron walked up to Trish's front door as if they were the Three Musketeers, one for all and all for one. Vicki knew their approach was risky, for Trish could have weapons and an entourage helping her, but Vicki doubted it. Although she and Byron were unarmed, she was certain that Aunt Mabel had a pistol in her purse and a switchblade tucked inside her bra.

Victoria whispered a prayer before giving Byron the signal to ring the doorbell. Ninety seconds later, Trish answered the door, wearing a short, silk, red robe and black flip-flops.

"Dr. Bliss?" she asked in surprise. "What-what are you doing here?"

Before Byron could respond, Aunt Mabel jumped in Trish's face and answered for him. "Little girl, I'm going to ask you one time and one time only. If you know what is good for you, you won't lie to my face. Did you kidnap Victoria's twin sister, Vivian?"

Trish gasped as if astonished. "What? Are you accusing me of kidnapping?"

Aunt Mabel sighed, and apparently unsatisfied with Trish's response, grabbed the woman's arm, and pulled it behind her back, putting her into a "chicken wing" position. She pushed the girl back into the house at the same time and said, "She's lying. Search the house, y'all."

"No! Get off–," Trish began to say, but was silenced by Aunt Mabel's stubby fingers over her mouth.

Vicki and Byron gawked at each other in shock, not knowing whether to follow Mabel's directions or get out of there and not be an accessory to a crime.

"I ain't got all day, y'all," Mabel said, breaking them out of their trance.

Vicki nodded and said, "OK. Byron, you look upstairs and I'll take this floor and the basement."

Byron glared at Mabel and Trish for a moment before running off deeper into the house to find the stairs. Vicki also began to head further into the house, but stopped in her tracks and glanced back at Trish. "Where is my sister?" she asked in an intimidating voice.

Trish's eyes became wide and she began to struggle harder against Mabel which instantly confirmed to Vicki that Vivian was somewhere in the house.

"Hurry up, child, before I have to knock her out!" said Mabel.

Vicki jogged through the living room into the kitchen, opening every door and looking in every space large enough to hold a human. After searching the entire downstairs area, she found the door to the basement, flicked on the light, and quickly dashed down the stairs.

Landing at the bottom step, she visually surveyed the dimly lit basement, and gasped when her eyes fell upon the shape of a body, sitting on a chair, tied to a pole in the middle of the room.

"Vivian!" she cried and ran toward the body. As she got closer, she noticed that it was indeed her sister, but her eyes were closed and she wasn't moving. "Vivian!" she screamed as she wiped tears away from her eyes and tried to shake her sister into consciousness.

A low groan came from her sister's body, and filled with hope, Vicki pulled the duct tape away from Vivian's mouth.

"Viv, it's me. It's Vicki. I'm here!"

Vivian slowly opened her eyes, and recognizing her sister, she said, "Vicki."

Vicki could hear the sound of Byron running on the first level and also calling out to her.

"Byron! Down in the basement! She's down here!" Vicki yelled back.

A few seconds later, Byron went flying down the basement stairs. He dashed over to the women and began helping Victoria loosen the rope around Vivian's hands and feet. By the time they freed Viv and helped carry her upstairs, Aunt Mabel had her switchblade up to Trish's throat, threatening to send her to meet her Maker.

"Aunt Mabel!" Vicki objected.

"This girl done kidnapped my niece. I hope she don't think she's getting away with it!"

"What are we going to do with her?" Byron asked.

At that moment, two police officers burst through the front door with David in tow.

"Put down your weapon!" they ordered Mabel, who looked at them angrily then dropped the switchblade, letting it thud against the hardwood floor.

"David, what are you doing here?" Vicki asked, excitedly.

David ran over to Vicki and Byron, removing his wife from their arms. "Byron called me and told me what you all were planning. Detectives Hernandez and Smith are old buddies of mine who've been helping me look for Viv unofficially until we could file the missing person's report today. But I guess all of that is unnecessary now." He looked into his wife's frightened eyes. "I'm so glad to see you, honey. Thank You, God, thank You."

"But what is going to happen to Trish?" Vicki asked. "She can't just go free. She's dangerous."

The detective, who had been identified as Smith, walked over to Trish and slapped a pair of handcuffs on her wrists. "Don't worry about her. We'll handle it from here. I hear you two have a wedding to attend in a few hours, so go and be with your family." Smith escorted Trish out of the house, leaving everyone else behind.

Hernandez chuckled and shook his head. "You all have a lot of guts. Technically, I would have to book you all too, for trespassing, but somehow our report will read that we stormed the house after finding just cause. Get your stories together; we'll stop by your house in the morning to get your statements."

Byron smiled deviously. "Could you make that tomorrow afternoon?"

Everyone laughed. "You got it. Congrats," Hernandez said. "And someone get that razor off the floor before it ends up getting tagged as evidence."

"Thanks," Vicki replied before bending over and retrieving Mabel's switchblade. "Well, you all heard the cops. It's time for a wedding!"

Yellow. Radiant yellow flowers decorated the church and Victoria's hair. The color filled the sanctuary with life and the beauty of summer in full bloom. Not an eye was dry in the church, not even Nancy's, who showed up and apologized for allowing envy to get the best of her. She admitted that seeing Vicki with Byron had resurfaced her longing to have someone special and caused her to distance herself from her good friend. Vicki accepted her apology quickly, conveniently forgetting to leave out the part where she thought Nancy had kidnapped her sister.

Vivian stood by Victoria's side like a proud older sibling. Upon leaving Trish's home, they had taken Viv to an urgent care facility, having her checked for injuries and dehydration. Luckily, she was given some fluids and a clean bill of health and permitted to attend the wedding.

Victoria and Byron gazed into each other's eyes as if no one else in the world existed. The days surrounding their wedding had been trying, demonstrating to them the complexity of fighting for love and the wonder of how strong love can truly be.

"Now by the power vested in me by the state of New York, I proudly pronounce you man and wife. You may now kiss the bride."

Byron wrapped his arm around his new wife's waist, dipped her as if they were dancing, and kissed her with the vigor of a man falling in love all over again.

About the Authors

A'ndrea J. Wilson, Ph.D. is the bestselling author of over a dozen books, including the novel *Wife 101*. She also writes thrillers and mysteries under the pen name **Janell**. For more information about her titles, visit her websites at www.andreawilsononline.com and www.iamjanell.com.

Kesha K. Redmon is the author of *On My Own* and moonlights as a toxicologist. She currently resides in Memphis, TN where she is working on her next project.

Vanessa Niki Davis is an up and coming writer. She obtained her B.A. in Creative Writing from California State University Long Beach. *Immortal Spring* is her first published work.